Haunt of the Nightingale

Haunt of

JOHN R. RIGGS

the Nightingale

A Garth Ryland Mystery

DEMBNER BOOKS • New York

DEMBNER BOOKS
Published by Red Dembner Enterprises Corp.,
80 Eighth Avenue, New York, N.Y. 10011
Distributed by W. W. Norton & Company, Inc.,
500 Fifth Avenue, New York, N.Y. 10110

Library of Congress Cataloging-in-Publication Data

Riggs, John R., 1945–
    Haunt of the nightingale / John R. Riggs.
    (A Garth Ryland mystery)

    I. Title. II. Series: Riggs, John R., 1945–   Garth Ryland
mystery.
PS3568.I372H38 1988   813'.54—dc19   87-30605
ISBN 0-934878-97-8

Design by Antler & Baldwin, Inc.

To Therese, who asks my best

Haunt of the Nightingale

1

On a Sunday afternoon in mid-December all good men and true should be inside watching the NFL game of the week. Axe in hand, I stood at the northeast end of Grandmother Ryland's farm where the white pine grew. A light gritty snow fell, dusting the ground and casting a white halo across the woods. I had thought I was alone until then.

Fresh, just a few minutes old, frayed at the edges where the wind had eaten it away, the footprint was otherwise perfectly preserved in a patch of new snow. A woman's footprint by the looks of it, or a child's; in any case, a small footprint compared to mine.

Kneeling, I looked for other footprints. Though they weren't as distinct as the first, I could make out a couple more. They led down a hill and into a ravine.

I glanced up at the pine I'd come to cut, watching the snow sift through its long green needles. In any season, when my life got too busy or too noisy or too important, I found peace and humility there among the pines. Maybe the fall of a single tree wouldn't change that. Maybe it would. Lacking omniscience, I shouldered my axe and walked down the hill into the ravine.

As a boy I'd once followed a fox as he made his rounds. Stopping where he stopped, pausing where he paused, I found all the things that attracted his attention and made the memories he would one day tell his pups. It was the same with the person I followed. At every turn I could see her eyes widen with the joy of discovery as she stopped to smell a sassafras, knelt to peer inside a hollow log, swung on a grapevine, chased a squirrel, drank from a spring. Like seeing life for the first time, she went from this to that with the unbridled energy of a child. And childlike, she never stopped to look behind her.

Her tracks led up to my barn and in the stable door. I didn't see any tracks leading out. I climbed the gate and dropped into the yard where Jessie was parked. Jessie was Grandmother Ryland's brown Chevy sedan, which she'd willed me along with the farm 6½ years ago. The farm was my reward for being her favorite, Jessie my punishment for not doing a better job of it.

Sliding the door open just far enough for me to squeeze through, I slipped into the barn and turned on the light. She stood facing me less than ten feet away. I didn't know which of us was more surprised.

"Hello," I said. "I'm Garth Ryland. I own this farm."

She didn't answer. Frozen with fear, she only stared at the axe I carried. I'd forgotten I even had it along.

"I'm sorry," I said, laying down the axe. "I came to cut a Christmas tree when I saw your tracks. I didn't mean to scare you."

She still didn't answer. Something about her said she wasn't going to. The long black coat that dragged the ground and looked several sizes too big for her, the pale white skin and chopped yellow hair that made her appear doll-like, the glassy look in her blue eyes, that of a young bird too terrified to run and too new to fly—all told of a past that was perhaps better left unspoken.

Leaving the axe lie, I backed up a step to show my good faith. "I'm leaving now," I said. "I might be back from time to time so don't worry about it. You're welcome to stay here as long as you like."

She continued to stand and stare without speaking. I'd backed all the way to the door and was about to close it when she rushed forward and picked up the axe. She held it in both hands

10

facing me. The way she held it, hands apart and feet spread for balance, left no doubt she knew how to use it.

I stepped outside and pulled the door closed. Then I got in Jessie and drove home.

Ruth Krammes, my housekeeper, met me at the back door. She was on her way out as I was on my way in.

"I thought you went after a Christmas tree," she said.

"I did, but something came up."

"Well, I don't have time to hear about it."

Ruth and I had been together ever since I bought the *Oakalla Reporter* and moved to Oakalla, Wisconsin, 6½ years ago. A big-boned Swede, she stood five foot-ten in her stocking feet and had grey-blond hair and a steely look and manner that kept Girl Scouts and Jehovah's Witnesses alike away from our door. We weren't the perfect couple. I was too stubborn. She was too opinionated. But somehow we got along.

"Where are you going?" I asked. Normally on a Sunday afternoon she was glued to the TV watching the Packers.

"Bowling."

"I thought that was Thursday."

"They moved it up because of the holidays."

"Then good luck," I said.

"We bowl our average we won't need it."

After Ruth left I called Chief Deputy Harold Clark, Clarkie as he was known to us around Oakalla. I would have called Sheriff Rupert Roberts, but he and his wife, Elvira, were in Omaha visiting Elvira's sister and family. I expected him back by the end of the week. With any luck Clarkie and I could keep a lid on things until then.

"Clarkie, this is Garth Ryland. I have a favor to ask."

"Name it."

Clarkie had never lacked enthusiasm. He lacked judgment. When it came to firearms, he couldn't hit the proverbial bull in the butt. And without Rupert to guide him he would have been lost. But as long as Rupert pointed him in the right direction, with his mile-a-minute energy there was no end to the things Clarkie could do, especially with his computer.

"I've got a description for you. I want you to run it through missing persons and see if you can come up with anything."

"Okay, fire away."

"White, female, age twenty-five to thirty, blond hair, blue eyes, height somewhere around five feet, weight a hundred pounds at most."

"Anything else?"

"Not that I can think of."

"My computer's on the blink right now. It might be tomorrow morning before I can run it through."

"That'll be fine. Call me when you do."

"Just out of curiosity, where is this person now?"

"My barn, I hope."

"You think she's a runaway?"

"From something. I don't know what yet."

"What's she doing in your barn?"

"That's what I'm trying to find out. She came from somewhere northeast of here, if that'll help you out any."

"There's a woman's prison in Spartansburg. That's northeast of here."

"Good guess, but I don't think so. She doesn't have that look about her."

"What kind of look does she have?"

"That's hard to describe, Clarkie. Someone might call it the living dead."

"But you don't?"

"No. But don't ask me why."

I hung up and went into the kitchen, where I began packing Ruth's picnic basket with all the leftovers I could find. Fried chicken, baked apples, pumpkin pie, and seven-layer salad went in, along with knife, fork, spoon, paper towels, aluminum foil, quart of milk, and a roll of toilet paper. I hesitated a long time before I threw in a box of matches. If I misjudged her, I might come back and find the farm burned down.

Before I left I went upstairs to my cedar chest and took out a couple of wool blankets. If the weather turned colder as it was supposed to, she would surely need these.

I doubled-checked the basket. I wished Ruth were around to tell me what I'd forgotten. Even more I wished Diana could ride out to the farm with me. She inspired trust in everyone she met. And she helped me simply by being there within reach.

Sliding open the barn door, I stood a moment in the doorway to let her know I was there. The last time I'd seen her she'd been holding an axe. That was reason enough to be cautious.

I turned on the light, half expecting her to still be standing where I left her. She wasn't. The axe was also gone. I set the basket down and left.

The snow, which had fallen intermittently all day, started up again, blowing across the road and running in eddies along its edge, but not sticking to the road itself. I came to Fair Haven Road and turned south toward Oakalla. Because my thoughts were elsewhere, I didn't see Will Cripe until I was nearly upon him. He stood at the edge of the road looking down into the side ditch. I slid to a stop beside him.

"Did you lose something?" I asked.

"Lucky," he answered. "I'm afraid he might have gotten hit by a car."

Lucky, Will's black Labrador retriever, a wide-muzzled, broad-chested old reprobate, was at least fifteen years old, and up until recently had the stamina of a mountain goat.

"I'll help you look," I said.

"Thanks. I appreciate it."

I parked Jessie in Will's driveway and walked back to where he stood. Will Cripe lived in the first house north of Fair Haven Church on the east side of the road. He'd built Fair Haven Church shortly after he returned from World War II, and while he'd gone on to build other churches, along with many of the houses in Oakalla, Fair Haven remained his favorite building. He once looked in on it daily and fixed whatever needed fixing. Lately, though, his visits had become more infrequent. Will Cripe had leukemia.

"Where have you looked?" I asked.

"From here to the house on this side of the road."

13

"I'll take the other side," I said. "I'll meet you at Skyler's Woods."

"Fair enough."

I crossed to the other side of the road and began searching the side ditch for Lucky. Will soon began to trail behind and gradually the distance widened between us. At Skyler's Woods I waited for him to catch up.

Once upon a time I wouldn't have had to wait. He would have waited for me. With his high cheekbones, aristocratic nose, and whip-like hammer and smile, he was Oakalla's paladin, the soft-spoken man in black who said little, shot straight, and did it all with ease.

He had been my idol. I'd framed my first house for him, earned my first real money from his pocket, shot my first goose from his blind. He taught me how to hold a hammer, how to swing an axe, where cranberries grew, and what wild rice looked like. Throughout it all he rarely spoke a word of praise or raised his voice in anger. He taught me by his cool grey eyes and tight-lipped smile that real men are strong and silent, and never cry no matter how much it hurts. I'd been a long time unlearning that lesson.

But I still respected him, still loved him with a love that was older than friendship. Watching him, leaden-legged and hollow-cheeked, bend into the snow, I could feel my last pillar of childhood about to fall.

"I didn't see him," I said when Will finally reached Skyler's Woods."

"Nor did I."

"Where do you think he might be?"

He nodded east in the direction of Willoby's Slough. "There."

"I was afraid you were going to say that."

We crossed a fence and started down a hill toward Willoby's Slough, a winding stretch of marsh that ran southeast toward Oakalla. A haven for ducks, pike, muskrats, and other wildlife, Willoby's Slough was not so hospitable to man. In summer a low dark cloud of insects hovered even on the brightest of days, and in winter hidden springs bubbled just far enough beneath the surface to keep the ice black and thin and treacherous.

But that had never kept me out of Willoby's Slough. In spring and summer I fished it, and in fall I hunted ducks until the first ice formed. Then I put on my skates and glided deep into its heart where no one else would go.

I'd never fallen through until three years ago, when the ice gave way and I nearly drowned, would have drowned if there hadn't been a beaver lodge nearby where I rested until help finally came. I hadn't been back in Willoby's Slough since. It seemed our long-standing pact had been broken. I no longer trusted it. It no longer welcomed me.

I tested the ice at the edge of the slough. Though it seemed solid, I hesitated to put my full weight on it.

"What do you think?" I asked Will.

"It'll hold you."

"I'm not so sure."

"Suit yourself."

He started out across the ice in search of Lucky. Reluctantly, I followed him. He'd gone only a short way when he stopped to stare at the ice.

"Find something?" I asked.

He didn't answer. His gaze lifted from the ice to sweep all of Willoby's Slough. He seemed more alert, more alive than he had for months.

I walked to where he stood. In a patch of snow was a small, perfectly-formed snow angel about the size of the woman who was in my barn. Like Will, I felt something come to life inside me.

"It looks like we're not the first ones here," I said.

Will still didn't answer. He continued to scan the ice, looking through and beyond me.

"No. Not the first ones," he finally said.

Then I heard a dog bark to the south of us. Will heard it, too, though he made no move in that direction.

"It sounds like Lucky," I said.

"Yes, it does."

"You going to him?"

"Why wouldn't I?"

Fortunately, Lucky hadn't gotten too far out on the ice before he fell down and couldn't get back up again. His tail thumped the ice weakly as we approached. Sorry guys, his eyes seemed to say, I'm not as young as I used to be.

"You old fool," Will said gently, kneeling to pat Lucky's broad head. "What are you doing out here?"

"He might have been chasing ducks," I said. "I saw a flock go over while I was at Grandmother Ryland's."

"Headed this way?"

"Yes."

A look of concern came over his face. "That means there's still open water out there somewhere."

I nodded. Somehow I'd known there would be.

Together Will and I carried Lucky off the ice and part way up the hill to Will's house. From there Lucky wobbled the rest of the way up the hill on his own, but when he reached the top, he could go no farther. Neither could Will by the looks of him, but he wouldn't admit it.

I carried Lucky across the yard and into the house, where I laid him in his bed beside the stove. Will arrived a short time later and took a seat at the kitchen table. He had to steady himself on the table before he sagged into the chair.

"Are you going to be all right?" I asked.

"Does it matter?"

"It does to me."

"I'm dying, Garth. Today or tomorrow makes no difference. I've got no family to leave behind and nothing left I want to do. Why make something hard that should be easy."

"What about Lucky?" I said. "You've got him."

Appropriately named, Lucky had been in and out of every kind of trouble known to dogs and had even invented some of his own. He'd been accused of everything from leveling Sissy Pickering's sunflowers to impregnating Beulah Peters' prize poodle on the steps of Fair Haven Church during choir practice. As with all legends, his feats were sometimes exaggerated, but in

Lucky's case not by much. He had more lives than a cat and more nerve than a high wire walker. I liked him because he was living proof that someone still looked after the scamps of the world.

"You need anything before I go?" I asked Will.

"You might put some water on to boil. A cup of tea sounds pretty good right now."

"What about supper?"

"I'll cross that bridge when I get to it."

"You're welcome to come home with me. We'll manage to scrape up something." Though the fried chicken and baked apples we'd had for dinner wouldn't be part of it.

"Thanks but no thanks. I'll manage."

I was at the door when I asked, "That snow angel we saw in the slough, did it mean something to you?"

"Why do you want to know?"

"Something came alive inside you when you saw it. At the risk of assuming too much, I'd call it hope."

"False hope, Garth. That's the story of my life."

"Then it has no special significance?"

"I didn't say that. It reminded me of someone, that's all. She was always doing something like that. She couldn't help herself. She loved life too much to just sit still and watch it happen. And she loved the slough nearly as much as Lucky."

"Did they ever roam the slough together?"

"Many times."

"What was her name?"

"Why do you want to know?"

"I'm just curious, that's all. It's off the record, if that's what you're worried about."

"Maybe some other day." He glanced up at me, his eyes keen. "I know you too well to tell you too much. I'd like to keep at least some of my secrets for myself."

"I can't argue with that."

He smiled. "No. But you'll try to find a way around it."

I stepped outside. It was still snowing, the hard little flakes gnat-like in the near dusk, stinging when they bit bare flesh. I pulled my stocking cap down over my ears and stuffed my hands in my pockets. The wind blew from the northeast, the direction from which the footprints had come.

Perhaps it wasn't ducks that Lucky had chased into Willoby's Slough. Perhaps it was a long-forgotten scent that tickled his nose and stirred his memory of days gone by. Perhaps he rushed to embrace it, then fell on the ice and couldn't get up. If so, if there were someone who could reawaken hope in Will Cripe and make his last days worth living, I had one more reason to find out who was hiding in my barn.

I drove home and called Clarkie. Nothing yet, but he was working on it. He promised to call me the moment he had something.

Pacing from window to window, watching the Christmas lights come on up and down the street, I realized I needed something to occupy my mind. But the house was too quiet to read, and without Ruth there to bet with, I didn't feel like watching football. I could always build a fire, but I didn't feel like that either.

I took a walk uptown, stopping to stare at the For Sale sign in Diana's yard as the dusk deepened and the snow continued to fall. Funny, her house was something I just assumed would always be there for me, a place where I could take off my shoes, build a fire, pop a bowl of popcorn for two, and sit down with a friend. Her house smelled and felt like home—home as I remembered it, home as I wanted it, with her at the heart.

But Diana was in Madison, studying at the University of Wisconsin while trying to discover where she went from there. Almost a blue-eyed blonde, with pale grey eyes, light brown hair, and a smile that turned me inside out, she'd come to a crossroad in her life soon after her husband Fran died and decided she needed to be on her own for a while. Ironically, she made her decision to leave Oakalla at the very same time I realized it had everything I ever wanted.

I turned my back on the For Sale sign, walked to the *Oakalla Reporter*, and sat down at my desk, which was oak, three feet wide and five feet long, built to last in a time when lasting was

18

important. Whenever I needed something solid to lean on, I went there.

I tried to call Diana and got a busy signal. That wasn't unusual. All I'd gotten lately were busy signals. When I tried again in a half hour and got another one, I stood and walked to the window. Barely visible, the snow fell as a white shadow.

I watched my breath steam the glass, then drew a heart there. When Diana and I used to make love, we'd take the phone off the hook. Sometimes for hours.

2

The sun peeked over the horizon, sent runners of light along the length of every tree and limb, ignited roofs and patches of snow, and burnt orange against the frost on the east window. Ruth stood at the stove frying bacon, wearing her blue house slippers and her flowered pink robe. The robe had belonged to her great-grandmother, the slippers to Martha Washington. I'd been racking my brain trying to decide what to get her for Christmas. Now I knew. The trick would be to get her to wear them.

"How did your bowling go?" I asked.

"We lost." I thought I heard her teeth gnash. Like me, Ruth was not a good loser.

"By how much?"

"Thirty-seven pins. We had them beat going into the last frame. All we had to do was mark. But Liddy Bennett had a seven-ten split, Wanda Collum threw two gutter balls, and Flo Fisher lost her grip on the ball and ended up in the next alley on top of Sarah Sue Peters. Nearly put both of them in the hospital."

"What happened to you?"

She broke the shell and plopped an egg into the hot bacon grease. I hoped that one was hers. "I missed the head pin."

"That doesn't sound so bad . . . considering."

"Twice." She plopped another egg into the grease.

"Well, at least you got nine pins."

"Which was ten pins below my average."

She banged around in the refrigerator for a couple of minutes, pretending to rearrange the shelves. Then she came to an abrupt halt. Puzzled, she set the half-and-half on the table in front of me.

"You raid the refrigerator yesterday?" she asked.

"Yes."

"Any special reason?"

I told her where the food went and why.

"You have any idea where she came from?" Ruth asked.

"Northeast, like I told Clarkie. It looked like she clipped the north end of Willoby's Slough on the way."

"What's to the northeast?" she thought out loud.

"Clarkie says there's a woman's prison, but I don't think she's an escapee. She doesn't have that look about her."

"What kind of look does she have?"

"Clarkie asked the same question. I told him that some might say the living dead, but I didn't think so. She's pale to the point of death and her eyes have a glassy look to them, but she sure moved fast enough when I dropped the axe."

"In what direction?"

"Toward it."

"Trouble," Ruth said. "That's what she looks like to me."

"She was scared. It was a natural reaction."

She gave me her all-knowing look. "I'll bet you next week's salary she's pretty too."

"I never noticed."

"Is that why your ears are turning red?"

The phone rang. I jumped at the chance to answer it. It was Clarkie.

"A woman by the name of Edith Gohler called in a missing persons report yesterday from Four Corners. It's a small town about twenty miles northeast of here."

"Yeah, I know where it is. Did she give a description?"

22

"Yes. It seems to match yours."

"Do you have an address?"

"402 Pretty Prairie Road."

"I'm on my way."

"Saved by the bell," Ruth said.

I smiled, but didn't answer.

Outside, it was near zero, one of those cold still mornings I remembered from childhood, when with rosy cheeks and teary eyes and seven layers of clothes weighing me down, I trudged off to school. Six blocks had seemed like six miles then. Lately it had seemed like ten.

As I raised the garage door, I already knew what was in store for me. It wasn't a simple case of will she or won't she start. After a night in the garage at four-above-zero, Jessie would take me to the limit before she finally decided.

I wasn't wrong. On her last amp of juice and my last drop of patience, she caught, sputtered, and finally started. Before she could change her mind, I roared out of the garage and into the alley, nearly running over my neighbor on the way. He waved and smiled. He'd been there before.

Four Corners sat on the edge of a seven-mile stretch of prairie that once grew foxtail, cattails, bluestem, and millet, and now grew corn and soybeans that stretched in nice neat rows as far as the eye could see. Except for an antique shop and a welding shop, both closed, there were no businesses in Four Corners. I stopped at the post office and asked for directions to 402 Pretty Prairie Road. The postmistress directed me to the east edge of town and told me I couldn't miss it. I smiled. I'd heard that one before.

But in this case she was right. Huge and Victorian and out of place on the edge of a prairie, Edith Gohler's house had a tower, three cupolas, and enough gables to keep Hawthorne in books for years to come. Once white, it had greyed through the years until only white peelings showed. Its concrete foundation had started to crumble. Its porch swing dangled by one chain, sawing to and fro in the prairie wind.

23

Edith Gohler was outside filling her bird feeder. A tall sturdy woman with a kind sad face and a double chin, she wore a long grey coat, rubbers, black leather gloves, and a small white hat. Her movements heavy and joyless, she scooped the seed from bucket to feeder, bucket to feeder, bucket to feeder.

"Work for the night is coming," I said.

She didn't look up. "Don't we both know it."

When she finished filling the feeder, she looked at me for the first time. Her eyes matched her face. They were kind and sad.

"You're not from around here," she said.

"No. I'm from Oakalla. My name is Garth Ryland. I publish the *Oakalla Reporter.*"

"A newspaper?"

"Yes."

"What is the news from Four Corners that would bring someone from Oakalla here?"

"A missing person."

"Of course. Mary. Have you found her or are you just looking?" There was no expression in her voice. Either she was afraid to hope or had forgotten how.

"That depends," I said.

"On what?"

"On why she ran away."

"Why don't you come inside."

I followed her around the house and through the back door into a large, unheated, boxlike room that was a catchall for everything from canning jars to mousetraps. She left her hat on, but put her gloves into the pocket of her coat and hung it on a wooden peg. She set her rubbers on the newspaper underneath. It was a yellowed copy of the *New York Times.*

A man's leather jacket and cap hung on the peg beside hers. She noticed me staring at it. "Leo's," she said. "Leo Gohler, my late husband. You might have heard of him."

"I have one of his paintings hanging over my fireplace."

"Which one?"

24

"I don't know. It's a barn."

"They were all barns," she reminded me.

"This is the barn that Jack built. It has a sky like I've never seen before. It's the essence of winter." And loneliness, I could have added.

"Yes," she said gently. "I remember it."

We went into the kitchen, which had a pantry at one end, sink and cupboards at the other, a rough pine table lodged against the south wall, and across from it the largest wood range I'd ever seen. But the range was cold and so was the kitchen, stirred by a draft that seemed to come all the way from the top of the tower. I knew then why Edith Gohler had left her hat on. Even the mounds of newspapers and magazines piled in every available space couldn't keep the draft at bay.

She took a seat at the table and lighted a cigarette. I took a seat at the opposite end near the pantry. A bottle of Johnnie Walker scotch sat on the table between us. I never drank before noon, but if she had offered me some to warm me, I would have taken it. She didn't offer, however, and I didn't ask.

"How do you know about Mary?" she asked.

"Yesterday I ran across someone in my barn who didn't belong there. One thing led to another and then led here."

"Describe her for me, please."

I did to the best of my ability, including the impression I had that she was not quite of this earth.

"Mary," she said in the same dull voice.

"Why doesn't that make you happy?" I asked.

"Nothing makes me happy, Mr. Ryland."

"Not even for Mary's sake?"

"No. Not even for Mary's sake. Because I'm not sure I want her back."

"She's not your daughter?"

"No. I don't know who she is, or if Mary is even her right name. I first met her five years ago when I was visiting Leo at Central State Hospital in Matom. She was such a lost little thing. She could never have survived on her own, which is

25

where she would have been when they released her. So I made the proper arrangements and brought her home with me."

Central State Hospital at Matom was a mental institution. Leo Gohler had been, by reputation, an alcoholic. Putting two and two together, I decided he must have been admitted there for treatment.

"Do you know any of Mary's history?" I asked.

"Very little. She had been at Central State about three years when I met her. In those three years she had never spoken one word. She still hasn't spoken since."

"Nothing?"

"Nothing. Until Saturday night."

"What happeend then?"

"I don't really know. Some carolers came by, children from the Methodist Church I think. All the outside lights were off. I don't know why they bothered to stop here, but they did. I was downstairs reading and Mary was up in the tower stargazing as she is wont to do. They were pitiful really. As Leo often said about me, they couldn't have carried a tune in a bucket. But they tried, dear hearts, and were singing "Silent Night" and what I hoped was their last song when this incredibly beautiful voice joined in and drowned out all the rest. I sat there mesmerized, quite shaken really. Then the carolers left and the house was silent. But I knew I'd just heard Mary's voice for the first time."

"What did you do then?"

"Nothing. She was down the stairs and out of the house before I ever recovered. She grabbed my old black coat on the way and her drawings and pencils. Little else that I can see. Perhaps her toothbrush and whatever else was handy."

"What was she wearing under the coat?"

"What she always wore. The green gabardine dress that had been my mother's. And tennis shoes, the only thing I bought her that she would ever wear." Edith Gohler smiled. It caught both of us off guard.

"You mentioned drawings and pencils. Where did those come from?"

26

Her smile faded. Rather, she seemed to banish it. "The pencils were Leo's. I gave them to Mary because Leo wanted her to have them. Leo knew her first, you see. She used to stand behind him and watch him sketch, from early on after Leo was admitted. He finally persuaded her to try her hand and was quite impressed with her talent. Monkey see, monkey do, was what I thought of it all until I brought her here and gave her the pencils. Leo was right. She had talent, though not as much as he."

"What did she draw?"

"Animals mostly. A few birds."

"No people?"

"None that I ever saw. There was, however, one drawing that came close. It had, if I remember right, a man's face on a dog's body. A disturbing drawing really. I found it hard to look at."

"I have the same trouble with centaurs."

"No. That wasn't it. Not the mixing of the two. It was the man's face, the bestiality I saw there. How, I thought, could this ever have come from Mary?" Her look, more than her words, told how much, even yet, the face horrified her.

"Did you ask her about it?"

"No. I didn't want her to know I'd been spying on her."

"You gave her the pencils. I wouldn't call it spying."

"You don't know Mary. She's not as dumb as she seems. She has her way of making her wants known, and one of her wants is to be left alone. I know. In the five years she was here, she never let me touch her."

"Did you try?"

"Once. She was in the tower, looking out across the prairie at something I couldn't see, the way Leo did sometimes when he'd been drinking. She had a strand of hair out of place. I merely reached down to right it and she nearly bit my finger off. After that I left her alone."

"Why do you think she bit you?" I asked, not sure I'd like the answer.

"Because I startled her, I suppose." Edith Gohler looked pensive, as if she feared the same thing I did. "Though I don't know why she reacted so strongly. I wasn't trying to hurt her."

"Maybe somebody once did. Hurt her I mean. Did she have the name Mary at Central State or did you give that to her?"

"She had it there."

"Do you know how she came by it?"

"No. Unless it was given to her by one of the staff."

"Do you have any photographs of her?"

"No. I'm sorry to say I don't."

"Any self-portraits?"

"If so, she took them with her."

I stared at Edith Gohler. Her cigarette had burned out, but she made no move to light another one. Apparently she wasn't a chain smoker, or a boozer either or she would have had a drink by now. She was obviously intelligent and well-read, with an insight into life most of us were still groping for. I couldn't feel sorry for her. She had too much dignity for that. But I had to wonder what had happened to all of her good intentions.

"Have I left anything out?" I asked.

"You said she's staying in your barn. You haven't told me what you plan to do with her."

"I don't know. Do you want her back?"

"I don't know, Mr. Ryland. I'm not sure but that Mary's time and mine has come and passed. I gave her shelter when she needed it. She gave me company if not comfort. As Leo was fond of saying, 'There's nothing more to do here.'"

"She can't stay in my barn forever."

"Then find her home . . . her real home. Perhaps she'll be happy there."

"Is this your real home?" I shouldn't have asked, but did.

"This was Leo's and my home. It's half my home now."

"I'm sorry I brought it up."

"Don't be. It was a fair question, seeing how I live. But you can also see there's nothing for Mary here. She was my ghost in the attic. Frankly, I'll be more comfortable now that she's gone."

She might have convinced me if, like Burl Ives, a little bitty tear hadn't let her down.

On the drive home I had a lot to think about. What bothered me most about my conversation with Edith Gohler was her description of the half-man, half-beast Mary had drawn. True, he lived in all of us, and in some more than others. But Mary saw him so vividly that she drew him in enough detail to horrify Edith Gohler. That made me wonder if he weren't real.

3

From my office I phoned Central State Hospital. They found Mary's records for me but had little to add beyond what Edith Gohler had already told me. Mary had been there three years before Edith Gohler took her home. No one knew where she came from or how she'd gotten the name Mary. Since she was a ward of the court, they suggested I start there. I had a better idea. I called the Wisconsin State Police and asked for Lieutenant Cavanaugh.

Lieutenant Fillmore Cavanaugh was, like Rupert Roberts, a good cop. He and Rupert had joined the state police together, after serving out their tour of duty as M.P.'s following World War II. I'd met him at Rupert's house, then seen him now and again when he was in town. We'd even drawn each other as partners one night when he, Rupert, Harvey Whitlock, and I got together to play euchre and swap stories.

"This is Garth Ryland," I said. "From Oakalla."

"How could I forget. You still calling trumps on the nine and the ten?"

"If I'm two-suited."

"With an ace on the side."

"Who said anything about an ace?"

"No wonder we lost. What's on your mind?"

"I need to know how one Mary Doe got to Central State Hospital eight years ago. She's a ward of the court, or was. They relinquished control over her five years ago. I wondered what she might have done to get admitted there."

"Why do you want to know?" He had a gruff voice that said, don't waste my time unless it's important.

"I believe she's here in Oakalla now. I'd like to get her home for the holidays."

"Is that a joke?"

"Yes and no. She's here, hiding in my barn. I just talked to her present guardian, but she's not sure she wants Mary back. Unless I can find her real home, relatives, parents, or otherwise, well, you can take it from there."

"Why bother me with it? If I remember right you've got a sheriff there." Then he added with a smile in his voice, "So I've heard, anyway."

"Rupert is in Omaha visiting relatives. Ever since he won the last election, we've had a hard time keeping him around."

"Prosperity will do that to you. I'll see what I can do."

"I appreciate it."

"But don't hold your breath. This isn't what I'd call a top priority case."

"I realize that. But there's still a life involved."

"Don't remind me of my job. That's what my chief is for. You say her name is Mary Doe and she was admitted to Central State eight years ago. Anything else?"

"No. That's about it. Leo Gohler taught her to draw, but I can't see where that's much help."

"Who's Leo Gohler?"

"A local artist. He was an alcoholic who only painted barns, but that's also irrelevant. Unless, of course, you happen to like barns. Some of us do."

On that, Lieutenant Fillmore Cavanaugh of the Wisconsin State Police hung up on me.

I spent the rest of the morning working on the *Oakalla Reporter*, stopping every few minutes to sit and stare out the window, then throw away the page I was on. This would be the Christmas edition and the last until the new year. I wanted it to be good. So far it wasn't.

32

After lunch at the Corner Bar and Grill, I stopped by home to see if there were any more leftovers before going to the farm. Ruth was one step ahead of me. She'd already packed them in a sack. I found it when I opened the door of the refrigerator.

I also found a note on the kitchen table telling me that Bill Nicewander had called to say my trusty Timex was fixed and ready to be picked up. The note also said that Will Cripe had called, though it didn't say why. Ruth had gone to Madison with Wanda Collum, but would be back in plenty of time to fix supper. She knew better than to turn me loose in her kitchen.

From a distance I saw someone bent over, walking slowly along Fair Haven Road. He appeared to be searching for something. Driving closer, I realized it was Will Cripe.

I stopped beside him. He opened the door and got in, then sat a moment to rest and catch his breath. It was hard to watch his struggle without assuming it.

"I'll be all right," he assured me.

"You couldn't prove it by me."

"I'm not trying to," he said quietly.

Minutes passed. With nothing else to do, I leaned back and closed my eyes. The sun felt good on my face.

"It's Lucky," Will finally said. "He's gone again."

"When?"

"Sometime in the night. He started whining and scratching at the back door, so I let him out, thinking he'd go about his business and come right back. He never did."

"You look in the slough?"

"As far as I was able. There's a lot of ice there, and not all of it's solid."

"He wasn't where we found him yesterday?"

"No. And nowhere else that I can see."

"Where could he have gone? You have any idea?" I asked.

"No. He's half blind and nearly deaf. About all he's got left is his nose. He might have been following it."

"Where?"

He didn't answer.

"Will? What aren't you telling me?"

33

He started to open the door. "Thanks for the heat, Garth. I'll be on my way."

"Ruth said you called."

"I did."

"Then you must have wanted my help."

He turned to face me. Though he was a shadow of his former self, his eyes had lost none of their power nor their fire. With one look, he could still make me feel like I was twelve years old.

"I wanted your help finding Lucky. That's all."

"Then you have it. Where do I start?"

"Wherever you want. I'm going to walk the road as far as Skyler's Woods, then back again."

"Why don't I start at the farm and work my way east. I have to go there anyway."

He opened the door and got out. "Fair enough. Stop by at home and let me know what you found." Then he forced a smile. "Who knows. He might already be there waiting for me."

"That's my bet," I said in reply. Though neither one of us believed it.

At the farm I filled a bucket with water from the well and went into the barn. My heart fell. The picnic basket sat where I'd left it. She hadn't even bothered to see what was in it.

That was my first thought. But when I picked it up I knew the basket was empty. My smile grew broad enough for all of Oakalla to see.

I glanced up at the hayloft. Mary should be there. She seemed more a being of the night than of the day, more at home in shadows than in the full light of the sun, and the dusky barn was the perfect place to wait for night to fall.

But there were footprints leading away from the barn toward Hoover's Ridge, a sand hill of cedar and scrub oak where, with typical boyhood enthusiasm, I had once dug up a cache of old bottles and, with typical boyhood stupidity, broken every one of them. On that same trip I'd discovered the abandoned house atop Hoover's Ridge.

Guarded by a gap-toothed windmill that creaked and

groaned every time it turned and, particularly at night when the wind was right, gave the ridge a ghostly sound, the house seemed to embrace the trees surrounding it as if part of the woods itself. Fascinated, yet fearful, I used to dare myself to go inside, then try to talk my way upstairs and back down again without running for my life. For years I never made it. If the windmill or a screech owl didn't get to me, my imagination would. When at last I did, I felt like I'd climbed Mount Everest.

Mary's tracks stopped at the doorway of the abandoned house. Large tracks, likely those of a man, as well as those of a dog, led inside. Lucky? It was a possibility. But to whom did the man's tracks belong?

Nothing smelled worse to me than a house gone to ruin. It did not yet belong to nature, but no longer belonged to man. Since neither claimed it, it festered and rotted and clung to life, even as time and the elements ripped it apart. Most of the floor had fallen through, and the ground beneath showed in several places. I weighed each step, trying to stay on the joists. It reminded me of yesterday's walk on Willoby's Slough.

At the first doorway I stopped to rest my nerves. I could smell skunk in the dirt beneath me, see rat holes in the floor and walls. A bird fluttered against a window, trying to find its way out, as something slow and furry crawled beneath the floor ahead of me. Then the bird came my way. I stepped aside to let it through.

I entered what I guessed was once a living room. A brick fireplace and chimney had held fast at the south end over the years and seemed to hold the rest of the house together. In front of the fireplace was a black leather chair that had nearly worn through to the springs. I stood for a long time looking at it. By the way its seat sagged and shone, it seemed someone had sat in it recently.

Something bumped the floor beneath me. "Lucky, you in here?" I asked.

No answer.

Kneeling to look under the house, I called to Lucky again. Had he been there, I was sure he would have barked.

35

I left the way I'd come and went outside into the sunshine again. Standing for a moment, I let the smell of the woods envelop me, hoping it would wash away the taste of the house. Then I started down a hollow in the direction of Will Cripe's, stopping every few yards to look and call for Lucky. If those were his tracks back on Hoover's Ridge, he was a long way from home. Chances were he wouldn't find his way back again without help.

I saw something black lying in the leaves ahead of me. "Lucky, is that you?" When he didn't answer, I went to him.

He lay on his side with his eyes closed and his front legs stretched out stiffly in front of him. His muzzle and paws were sandy from where he'd been digging in the dirt. He smelled faintly of skunk.

Kneeling beside him, I rubbed his chin and scratched his ears for the last time. His fur was warm from the sun. Trailing my hand across his broad head, I let it rest there a moment. It was then I noticed a knot that was sticky with blood. I could almost feel Lucky wince as I touched it.

Rising, I looked around the hollow, saw nothing that would tell me where the knot came from. If Lucky had tangled with a skunk, win or lose he would smell a lot worse than he did. If he had fought with something else, he would have some bites and scratches on him as well as the knot—unless, of course, he had tangled with a man.

4

I left Lucky in the hollow and continued across country toward Will Cripe's house through Fair Haven Cemetery. There I noticed the familiar figure of Reverend Sommerville Cooper standing beside his car in the churchyard. He appeared to be having trouble so I went to him. Knowing how Will felt about Lucky, I was in no hurry to tell him the bad news.

"Problems?" I asked.

Reverend Cooper gave me an exasperated look. He held a screwdriver pointed at the hood of his car, a purple De Soto that was nearly as old as Jessie. "I wonder, Garth," he said, "if the Lord is testing me."

"Somebody, anyway."

Reverend Sommerville Cooper and I had met six months before, soon after he'd come to Oakalla to take the Fair Haven charge. I was walking east along the north side of Jackson Street. He was walking west along the south side of Jackson Street. He crossed the street just as soon as he saw me. We met in front of Norma Rothenberger's house.

"Morning, neighbor," he said. "Isn't it a glorious day!"

As a matter of fact, it was a glorious day. "Yes," I answered.

"And aren't you Garth Ryland, publisher of the *Oakalla Reporter?*"

"Yes," I admitted. "I am."

"It's a fine paper. Reading it, I can see you are a religious man."

"By whose definition?" Because I wanted to think that myself.

He ignored my question. "But also a skeptical one," he continued. "Don't you believe there are some things we can take on faith alone?"

"Yes. But religion isn't one of them."

He smiled, welcoming the challenge. "I can see we have some work to do, you and I."

"If you can keep up with me."

"I believe I can."

That had been our first meeting. It wasn't our last. Reverend Sommerville Cooper, Coop as I'd come to call him, took me on as his personal mission. Whenever I looked around, there he'd be a few steps behind. At first it annoyed me. Then I began to see the humor in it. Finally, after I misled him right on up to the bar at the Corner Bar and Grill where he reddened but held his ground, we came to an understanding. He wouldn't try to convert me. I wouldn't throw tacks on the sidewalk every time I saw him coming. After that we became friends.

"What's the problem?" I asked.

"It'll start, but when I try to go somewhere, it dies on me," he said. "Here, I'll show you."

He showed me. As the De Soto kept dying, Coop's ruddy face became redder and redder until he looked like he was going to explode. He was a big man with a big voice and a large head, made larger by a great puff of snow-white hair, so when the explosion came, it wouldn't be a small one.

"Let me try it," I said, trying to defuse him a little.

"Gladly."

He got out and I got into the De Soto. I tried and got the same results.

"It acts like your fuel pump's going out," I said. "You'll probably have to call Danny at the Marathon and have him come after you with his wrecker."

I could tell by his scowl he didn't like that idea. Coop could pinch a penny about as hard as Ruth, and that was hard enough to melt the copper.

"I've got a chain in my trunk," he said. "Is your car handy?"

"She's over at the farm. But I've got some things I need to do first. It might be a while."

"I'm in no hurry. There's always something for me to do here. Just give me a holler when you get back."

"Will do."

Will Cripe stood on his front porch waiting for me. He looked like he'd been standing there a long time, like a sentry, watchful and patient, who had learned to put duty above self.

"He's dead, isn't he," Will said before I even had a chance to speak.

"Yes. He's dead."

"Where is he?"

"The first hollow this side of Hoover's Ridge."

Will was surprised. "What was he doing way over there?"

"I was hoping you could tell me."

Will shook his head. He didn't have an answer.

"You have a shovel handy?" I asked. "And a pick. I'll probably need it to break through the frost."

"You going to bury him there?" he asked.

"Unless you have a better place."

"What about the slough? We could cut a hole in the ice, weigh him down, and slide him in. He'd be happier there . . ." He lost his voice, then turned away to wipe his eyes, "than a damned holler somewhere."

"He'll find the slough no matter where we bury him. No one's going to keep him out."

Will nodded, then said bitterly, "I wish to hell I could join him."

"The shovel in the basement?"

"Yeah. The pick should be down there somewhere, too."

I went into the house and down to his workshop in the basement, where I found the pick and shovel, both covered with rust. Will once told me that "you can pretty well judge a man by the way he keeps his tools." That was why he always kept his clean, sharp, and oiled, and made me do the same. He also had another saying: With the right tool you can fix anything. I was still looking for the tool that would fix Will Cripe.

"You want to go along?" I asked.

He shook his head. "No. I don't think I could stand it."

I nodded. I understood.

"How did he die, Garth?" Will asked before I could get away.

"I don't know. At this point I don't want to guess."

"What do you mean by that?" His eyes skewered me, exerting their old power.

"It means I'm not as smart as I used to be. Twenty years ago I had all the answers."

"Didn't we all?"

I left him standing on the porch while I went to bury Lucky.

"Bury him deep, Garth!" Will shouted after me. "I don't want some varmint digging him up."

At Will's request I buried Lucky deep in the hollow where I'd found him, then used a granite boulder to mark the spot. Part of me wanted to tarry, recount some old memories, maybe shed a few tears, but Reverend Sommerville Cooper was waiting for me to drag him home. Taking the pick and shovel, I stopped by the farm long enough to put them in Jessie's trunk, retrieve the picnic basket, and hang Grandmother's tin drinking cup inside the barn door where Mary would find it. Then I drove to Fair Haven Church.

Coop was waiting for me in his De Soto, still trying to get it to go. Apparently even preachers ran out of things to do at church.

We hooked up the chain, and I drove slowly back to Oakalla, with Coop and the De Soto trailing along behind. Despite how I felt, I had to smile at the irony. For the first time since I'd owned her, Jessie was on the business end of the chain. I could see her smoking as she plotted her revenge.

Coop didn't like it when we had to leave the De Soto at the Marathon. His scowl deepened on the way to his house. Something troubled him that went beyond his car.

40

"You have a minute, Garth?" he asked when I stopped in front of his house.

I looked at my wrist, saw my watch wasn't there, and remembered that I was supposed to pick it up today. "What time is it?"

He looked at his watch. "A little after four."

"I have a minute." But I'd have to be at the jewelry store by five.

Coop lived in the Fair Haven parsonage, a small yellow frame house that sat on a half lot, squeezed between Sadie Jenkins' grey Victorian house on one side and Minnie Paul's grey Victorian house on the other, like a canary between two elephants. I had been inside the house once as a boy and once as an adult. Neither visit left a lasting impression.

I followed Coop inside, took off my jacket and cap, and sat down at one end of an overstuffed yellow couch. It was close in there and about ten degrees warmer than I kept my office, which at sixty-five was three degrees warmer than Ruth kept the house.

While Coop went after something, I looked around the small living room. The walls were paneled, the floor carpeted, the windows curtained. An orange light hung by a gold chain from the ceiling. A mock fire burned in a mock fireplace, but the musket hanging above the fireplace looked real.

"Is that old?" I asked on Coop's return.

"Is what old?" he replied.

"The musket."

"No. I made it just last year. For stillboard shooting."

"Where was that?" The last stillboard shoot in Oakalla had occurred years ago.

"Ricelander. That's where I was before I came here."

"Somehow I thought you came from the South." Ricelander was in northern Wisconsin. Coop didn't talk nor act like a native.

"I was born and raised in Kentucky. Maybe that explains it."

Coop stood uncomfortably in front of the mock fireplace. I sat uncomfortably on the edge of the couch. Our friendship, like a lot of others I'd known, worked best outside the home. It might

41

have helped if he'd offered me a drink of something, but he wasn't used to entertaining. As a minister, he was used to being entertained.

"What's on your mind?" I asked. I noticed he was holding something that he was reluctant to let go of.

"It's this." He handed me a letter that carried an Oakalla postmark. "I got it just this morning."

"You mind if I read it?"

"No. As long as it ends here."

"It will." I promised him.

Dear Sommerville Cooper,

You are an imposter, no more able to do God's work than a dog. My patience with you has run out.

You Know Who I Am

I looked from the letter to Coop. His normally ruddy face had deepened to purple. He was angry and embarrassed.

"You know who sent it?" I asked.

"No. I have no idea."

"Do you have a guess?"

"No. If I did, it wouldn't be proper to relay it to you."

He began to slowly pace the room, more troubled than I'd ever seen him. "God has called me to Fair Haven Church. He *knows* the good I can do there. But something keeps resisting me . . ." He stopped his pacing to look my way. "As if there is a conscious force opposing me. As if . . ." He hesitated because he didn't want to admit it. "As if Satan were at work there."

"In whose person?"

He avoided my question. He had a guess, but didn't want to tell me who it was.

"I don't know, Coop. Fair Haven isn't what it used to be. But by and large its people have been and still are a decent lot. I wouldn't sell them short."

He walked over and took the letter from me, reading it

42

again for probably the hundredth time. As he did, his anger flared. "Then how do you explain this?"

"I can't. I don't know anyone at Fair Haven mean enough to write it. Think it, yes, but not write it and send it to you."

"Someone did."

"I can't argue with that."

"So what am I supposed to do about it?"

"Ignore it and go on, the way I do whenever I get a crank letter. I figure I must be doing something right or I wouldn't have made somebody mad."

He couldn't let go of it so easily. "But have you ever gotten a letter such as this, one that makes you question your whole being and purpose?"

"I don't need a letter to do that. On my block it comes with the territory."

"Not on mine. I've always been certain of my path."

"Then you're among the lucky ones." I stood and stretched. The room was small and stuffy. It, along with Coop's righteousness, was starting to close in on me. "Let me know if you need a ride anywhere."

"Walk among fire, expect to get burned," he said. "That's it, isn't it? Why should I be different."

"That's it, Coop. We all have our crosses to bear."

"Some of us more than others."

I shrugged and left. He was probably right about that.

Ruth had taken my watch to the jewelry store with the fervent hope that it had seen its last tick. Not that she minded the watch so much, it was seeing me wind it for five or more minutes twice a day that drove her to distraction, especially since it was supposed to be self-winding.

Paul Peters leaned on a display case, looking like a bored aristocrat. Unmarried, somewhere in his mid-thirties, with slender hands and a deep voice that always sounded to me like God calling, Paul lived with his mother, Beulah Peters, in the west end of town. An excellent pianist, he played regularly at the Fair Haven Church and on rare occasions gave recitals at his

43

home. Though I liked Paul, I didn't count him among my friends.

"Afternoon, Paul." I noticed ugly yellow splotches that looked like old bruises under both his eyes. "What happened to you?"

He stifled a yawn. "You mean you hadn't heard? I fell down the basement steps at Fair Haven Church."

"No. I hadn't heard. When was that?"

"A couple weeks ago. On a Wednesday, I believe."

"Were you hurt badly?"

Though he tried to hide it with another yawn, his impatience with me was starting to show. "No. Not badly. Just my pride is all." He straightened, pushing himself away from the display case. "Now what may I do for you?"

"I came to pick up my watch. Ruth left me a note saying it was ready."

Paul walked stiffly to the back of the room and retrieved my watch. "Bill left me a note telling me the same thing."

Bill Nicewander, the owner, loved the jewelry business as much as Paul disdained it. I had to wonder why Paul continued to work there.

"Was there anything else?" Paul asked, handing me my watch.

"How much?"

"Ten dollars for cleaning it, I believe he said."

I took out a ten dollar bill and gave it to him. As he reached for the bill, I noticed he winced in pain. It seemed more than his pride had been hurt in his fall.

"Fair Haven Church, you say?"

He looked at me, like he were thinking the same thing. "What about it?"

"That's where you fell. Fair Haven Church?"

"Yes. Fair Haven Church."

"I was just out there today."

"Imagine that. So was I."

"What were you doing there?" I asked.

"Does it matter?"

44

"If it didn't matter, I wouldn't ask."

"Looking for someone. But I never found her." Immediately he wanted to take back his last statement, but it was too late.

"*Her?*" I asked.

"Annie," he admitted. "Annie Lawson."

"I don't know her."

His face showed the first real emotion I'd ever seen there. "Your loss," he said. Then I watched his hands close slowly into fists. "And mine."

"Do you care to explain that?"

He began to retreat, back to his old diffident self. "No, Garth, I don't."

5

I patted Jessie's fender when I got home, and told her what a good car she'd been. Ruth was in the kitchen fixing supper. It smelled good in there, especially after coming in from the cold. The way the temperature had been dropping since sunset, I expected it to be below zero by morning.

"You're back," I said, taking a seat at the kitchen table.

"In record time," she answered. "Wanda only dragged me through three malls and a K MART today. I got her out of there before she got her second wind."

"She buy anything?"

"What do you think? The way that car of hers was loaded, we looked like a circus wagon coming back. And she only got through half her Christmas list."

"She has a big family."

"No bigger than mine. She just thinks more of hers than I do."

I sat for a while without saying anything, taking in the smell of supper and letting the warmth of the kitchen seep into me. The kitchen was by and large my favorite room in the house. It seemed more friendship came out of it than anywhere else.

"I got my watch," I said, showing it to her. "Thanks for your note."

"Did he fix the self-winder on it?"

"No. He just cleaned it. I told him before I didn't mind winding it."

"Just do it out of my sight, that's all I ask."

"I'll try to remember."

"See that you do."

"Paul Peters told me he fell down the basement steps at Fair Haven Church."

"That's the story." Ruth was cutting homemade noodles for supper. "Why?"

"A lot seems to be happening out Fair Haven way lately."

"Such as?"

"Paul Peters for one. Mary, the woman in my barn, for another. Then Lucky, Will Cripe's dog, took off in the night, and I found him dead in a hollow not too far from Fair Haven. It looked like somebody might have killed him."

Ruth stopped cutting noodles long enough to look at me. "Why would somebody do that? Though God knows probably each and every one of us has a reason."

Lucky's reputation wasn't just confined to the Fair Haven area. Since Will had often taken him along when he was on a job in town, Lucky was equally infamous in Oakalla.

"Why would somebody send Sommerville Cooper a letter saying he was no more a preacher than a dog?" I asked. "That doesn't make any sense either."

"Who sent him that?"

"I don't know. Like I told him, I can't think of anybody from Fair Haven mean enough."

"Then you didn't look very hard."

"Meaning who?"

"You know who I mean. She drives a white Cadillac."

I knew whom she meant, Beulah Peters, Paul Peters' mother. Beulah was a large determined woman who tried, and usually succeeded, to run every show in town. She and I had butted heads a couple times, ending in a draw. She and Ruth wouldn't walk the same sidewalk if either saw the other coming. In Beulah Peters, Ruth had met her match; in Ruth, Beulah had met hers. Though even under penalty of death, neither would admit it.

"I agree Beulah is brassy and pushy," I said. "But I never thought of her as mean."

"Think again. When she and Chicken Coop get together, the sparks are bound to fly. They bring out the worst in each other, and there's plenty of that to go around."

She had a point. When Coop and Beulah had hooked horns over who should run Fair Haven Church, it was like two old water buffaloes going at each other. Sissy Pickering, who lived out that way, said she could hear the thunder of their battle from her house.

"I still don't think Beulah would snipe at him with a letter," I said. "If she had something to say to Coop, she'd say it to his face."

"Then give me your version." Finished with the noodles, she lifted the lid on the beef to see how it was doing.

"I was up on Hoover's Ridge earlier today . . ."

"What were you doing there?"

I suddenly flushed. "That's not important. What is important is that it looks like somebody might be staying at the old house."

She stopped stirring the beef. "Living there?"

"I wouldn't go that far. The house just looks used, that's all."

"What does that have to do with anything?"

"I think whoever's using it might have killed Lucky."

The phone rang. Ruth answered it. "For you," she said.

"Who is it?"

"A Lieutenant somebody from the State Police."

"Lieutenant Cavanaugh?"

"Why don't you ask him." She handed me the phone.

"Yes, Garth Ryland here."

"Who was that who answered the phone?"

"My housekeeper, Ruth Krammes."

"She always like that?"

"About. You were lucky. You caught her on a good day."

"Remind me to call your office after this."

"What do you have for me?"

"Not much. The trooper who brought Mary Doe in is now dead. You might remember him. His name was Ralph Coombs."

"I remember him." I also remembered that he'd died in the line of duty when he'd gone into an icy stream to try to save a kid from drowning.

"Anyway, Ralph filed a report and we have it here. It says in part he found her walking along State Road 13 in Adams County. She didn't know where she was or how she got there. When he asked her name . . . ," Lieutenant Cavanaugh was reading to himself, "'she didn't respond.'"

"That could mean that Mary's not her right name."

"It's a possibility."

"Go on," I said.

"He 'took her to the hospital where she was treated for facial contusions, concussion, and possible skull fracture. . . .'"

"What hospital?" Without realizing it, I'd started pacing back and forth in and out of the kitchen. Ruth's look told me to light somewhere.

"Wait a minute. There's more. 'Victim was dirty and disoriented, apparently suffering from shell shock.' Those are his own words."

"Why would he use the term shell shock?" Something had just clicked, like the first tumbler of a combination lock, but I couldn't take it further.

"I don't know. Ralph, like some of the rest of us, saw a lot of action during World War II. Maybe that's as close as he could come to it. He's got another military term in here somewhere . . ."

With one eye on me, Ruth stirred the noodles into the beef while Cavanaugh searched for it.

"Here it is at the bottom of the report. 'Foxhole?' I guess that was more or less a note to himself."

"Anything else?"

"No. That's about it. He took her to Portage County

50

Hospital, so it must've been the north end of the county where he found her."

"Do you think it'd do any good to call up there?"

"No. I've just been that route. Once they treated her injuries, she ended up in Winona at the psychiatric ward and from there she went to Central State. You know the rest of the story."

"Everything and nothing." I couldn't hide the disappointment in my voice.

"So goes life, especially in this business. You want frustration, be a real cop for a while."

"It seems I've heard that somewhere before." From Rupert about five hundred times.

"Good luck on this one. You'll need it."

"Thanks for taking the time to find out what you did. I know most of it was your own time."

"All of it was my own time. But, hey, it's Christmas, right? What else is there to do?"

"Exception-making," I said.

"Come again?"

"Someone once said that love is exception-making. You must love your job."

"No more than you do yours. Keep me posted on Mary. I'd like to know how she turns out."

"I will. Thanks."

Supper included the beef and noodles, which I put over my mashed potatoes, shell-out beans, and butterscotch pudding for dessert.

"What about leftovers?" I asked, pouring us cups of coffee.

"What about them?"

"I can't make any friends with cold mashed potatoes and cold beef and noodles."

"Who's trying?"

"I am."

"Why don't you bring her here? It'd be a lot easier to feed her."

51

"I would if I could. Now I'm lucky to get within a hundred yards of her."

"When the time comes, she'll have something to eat. I'll see to it."

I smiled at her. "You know, Ruth, you're not half bad."

"Flattery won't get you out of the dishes."

"Too bad. I was hoping something would."

"You ready for my help yet?"

"On what?"

"How Mary ended up on State Road 13."

If anyone could help, she could. Ruth and her relatives had a communications network that not even they knew the extent of. Every time they thought they'd reached its end, a long-lost cousin would turn up. Just this past year they'd added Alaska and the Virgin Islands.

"If you're offering," I said.

"I am. Where do you want me to look?"

"Wherever you want. Just be discreet. I don't know that Mary's in danger, but she might be."

"You have a reason for saying that?"

"Just a hunch for now. It has to do with Lucky's death and one of Mary's drawings Edith Gohler told me about. But if you want a reason, think about where she's been, then ask yourself how she got there."

"It could have been any of a hundred ways.

"Agreed." I said. "But how many of them are good?"

The phone rang. Ruth normally beat me to it, but at that moment she didn't have her running shoes on.

"Yes?" I asked.

There was no answer, even though I could hear someone breathing on the other end.

"This is Garth Ryland. Who is this?"

Still no answer. But I didn't think the person on the other end was playing games with me. It was like a child had dialed for help and now didn't know what to say.

"Mary, is that you? Do you need help?"

I heard a sigh. Then whoever it was hung up.

"Damn!" I said, putting down the receiver.

"What's the matter?"

"Someone just called. But she wouldn't say who it was or why she called. I think it was Mary and I think she's in trouble."

"Your barn have a phone?"

"No. Why?"

"If it was Mary, where did she call from?"

"Not the house. It's locked. Besides that, the phone's out of order. Fair Haven Church maybe. It's close and it's usually not locked."

"Why don't you call Will Cripe to see if he can see a light on there at the church? It might save you a trip."

"Good idea."

When after fifteen rings Will didn't answer, I knew he wasn't going to.

"I'm on my way," I said to Ruth.

"Call me if you need anything."

Jessie didn't want to start, but she finally did. I first drove to Fair Haven Church, but seeing no light there or anyone about, I went on to Will Cripe's.

Stepping from Jessie's semi-warmth into the crystal-black night, I realized why she had been so reluctant to leave the garage. It was cold. Close to zero, I guessed. Cold enough to burn my cheeks and make my eyes water, and press down with an icy thumb on my brow.

A light shone in Will's living room, but when I knocked on the back door, he didn't answer. I walked to a window and looked in. Will sat in his reclining chair. Wearing a bulky black sweater, he had an afghan pulled over his lap and tucked around his legs. He didn't appear to be reading or watching television. Nor did he appear to be sleeping. He seemed only to stare at the wall across from him, as if he had gone all cold inside and nothing he said or did made a damn bit of difference anymore. He seemed to be waiting for death.

I went in the back door to the living room. Will looked up at me, but didn't speak. His face was sallow and drawn, with deep pits in his cheeks from which the stubble of his beard jutted like a forest of drowned trees. His eyes had sunk far back into his head and looked barely alive.

"Will, are you all right?"

He didn't answer. The pupils of his eyes were huge. They made his eyes look black.

"Are you all right?" I repeated.

Again he didn't answer.

In the past he and I had passed the brandy bottle back and forth while fishing through the ice for bluegill on Grandmother's pond. We never did catch many fish, but then that's not what we went for.

I searched the kitchen cabinets and found the brandy in the bottom of his dry sink. Thick dust covered the bottle. Had it been that long ago?

After taking a glass from the cupboard, I filled it half full of brandy. "Drink it," I said.

He looked at me like he hadn't heard.

"Drink it or I'll pour it down you."

His eyes came to life. "Try."

I pinched his nose until his mouth opened, then poured in all the brandy I could. He sputtered and spat and knocked the glass from my hand, but I managed to get some brandy down him. Pitching forward, he coughed violently as color crept back into his cheeks. I went back for the brandy bottle and two more glasses.

I poured some brandy in each and handed one to him. I raised mine in a toast and drank from it. He just held his.

"What are we celebrating?" he asked.

"Life."

"You have to do better."

"Love?"

"Try again."

"Friendship."

His gaze traveled to the foot of the fireplace where Lucky's rug lay. "Okay. I'll drink to that."

I joined him. The brandy soon took hold, replacing the

54

chill of the night with a glow. I looked at the fireplace. It would look better with a fire in it.

"Does that thing work?" I asked.

"It did last week."

"You mind if I build a fire?"

"Help yourself. There's wood out back."

After laying a fire, I opened the damper and burned a couple sheets of newspaper by themselves to get the chimney to draw. It was something Will had taught me. Then, using one balled-up sheet of paper at a time, the way he'd also taught me, I started the fire. When I had it going, I carried in enough wood to last the night.

"That should hold you," I said.

"Aren't you staying?"

"For now. Tomorrow is another day."

"For some of us," he said quietly.

I didn't know what to say so I didn't say anything.

We watched the fire awhile. It drove every shadow from the room and put a light in every window, and for the moment held the night at bay.

"Why didn't you let me die?" Will asked.

"Because you still have some fight left in you."

"Not much."

"More than you know."

The fire gradually burned down. Above it, Will's .30-.30 Winchester, which had always hung over his hearth, began to fade from sight. How many years had it been since he and I stood at his back door, trying to sight it in? Too many, it seemed, to ever recall.

I got up to feed the fire. As I did, I thought I saw someone at the north window. But when I walked over to look, no one was there.

I walked back to the fireplace and began adding wood. "You didn't by any chance try to call me earlier this evening, did you?" I asked.

"No. I haven't moved from this chair."

55

"I just wondered. Someone did. That's why I came out here."

"They told you I was dying?"

"No. They didn't say anything."

"Then how did you know where to look?"

"I didn't. I just got lucky." I smiled at him. "Is it possible you have a guardian angel?"

"Not that I know of." But I could tell he was wondering himself.

"Is it possible someone could have come by here last night?" I asked. "That Lucky backtracked him for a distance, then lost his way?"

"It's possible," he admitted. "But not likely."

"How likely is it that someone would call me on your behalf tonight? It's close to zero out there. Who would walk a mile in it just to look in on you?"

Tears started to form in Will's eyes. He blinked them back. "Wasn't it time you were going?" he asked.

"If you want. You going to be all right?"

"What if I said no?"

"Then I'd stay."

"No. There's no need for that. I'll make it tonight at least. Tomorrow we'll have to see."

"I'll check in on you to see how it's going."

"Don't make it too early."

"What have you got planned?" I asked.

"Never mind. Just don't make it too early."

I put on my jacket and stocking cap. Will's voice stopped me at the door.

"Did you bury him deep?"

"I buried him deep. I'll get your pick and shovel back to you one of these days."

"There's no hurry," he said with the trace of a smile.

Drained by the cold, Jessie barely had enough spark to fire. When I reached Fair Haven Church, I left her running while I got out. I knew the door would be unlocked. It was one of the things Coop insisted on, that the door to salvation be kept open

56

at all times. It was also one of the things on which he and Beulah Peters disagreed.

I turned on the lights and stepped into the sanctuary, hesitated a moment to let the chill pass through me. Dark pews, a shade darker than walnut, altar and pulpit a deep rust, choir chairs aligned in neat rows of black—all combined to suck the light from the sanctuary and give it the look of a crypt.

This wasn't the church that Will Cripe had built. His had been spacious and filled with light. As a boy I used to love to come when no one else was here, sit where I could watch the morning sun stream through the stained glass window, and wool-gather to my heart's content. Cool and friendly and new, Fair Haven was the perfect summer church.

But time and cheerless minds had stained the pews and altar, then rearranged things to better suit themselves. Something else, too, more sinister than spite, more insidious than time, seemed at work. Like Coop, I'd felt its presence lately whenever I went in there.

Someone had been in Coop's office. Damp smudges led in and out of the room. I found a puddle of water beside the phone.

From the office I went down the back stairs to the basement. It, too, had darkened and dampened over the years and wore the faint scent of sewer gas. I called out to Mary, but she didn't answer.

Climbing the front stairs to the vestibule, I thought I heard someone walking in the church above me, but again when I called, no one answered. If it were Mary, I didn't want to press her too hard or I might scare her away. So I turned off the lights and left.

On the way out the drive I saw the church lights wink at me. I had to smile. Edith Gohler was right. Mary wasn't as dumb as she appeared. She had more than one way of making herself heard.

At home Ruth had just settled into her chair with one of the three hundred magazines she subscribed to. "What was that all about?" she asked.

"Will Cripe almost died tonight, though he's okay now. But

57

if Mary hadn't called me when she did, he probably would have died."

"How did she know to call you?"

"That's the easy part. I'd told her my name. Besides, it's there on the mailbox at the farm. What I don't understand is, one, what she was doing at Will's house, and two, how did she know where the phone was in Fair Haven Church."

"It does make you wonder, doesn't it."

"That's not all. I think Lucky might have been backtracking her when he was killed today. Then tonight I'm almost sure she came back to Will's house while I was there, then followed me to the church. For a stranger, she sure seems to know her way around."

"Maybe she's not a stranger," Ruth suggested.

"That was my next thought. You have any ideas?"

"No. But then I really haven't thought about it."

"I left her there in the church," I said. "I'm not sure that was a good idea."

"Why not?"

"Because of what happened to Lucky today."

"You're sure somebody killed him? That he didn't just die of old age?"

"I felt the knot on his head where something had struck him. The blood was still tacky . . ."

"And?"

"Something else. But it escapes me now."

She opened her magazine, but didn't start to read. "You say Lucky was backtracking Mary when he was killed?"

"I think so."

"Any chance she killed him?"

"There's always that chance. Though I don't want to believe it."

"Maybe to be on the safe side you should believe it. What do you really know about her except what you want to?"

"I know she saved Will Cripe's life tonight."

"You saved Will Cripe's life tonight. Don't give her more credit than she's due."

58

"I don't think that's possible."

She looked down at her magazine and started to read. "Romantics," she muttered. "You and Karl both."

Hours later Ruth sat nodding in her chair, while I was watching the fire I'd built. With my nose near the hearth I could smell the cedar log, its scent warm and familiar and very much at home. It made me think of Diana, how much I missed her and how badly I wanted her there, especially at that moment.

So when Ruth's magazine fell and her eyes closed, I took the opportunity to call. Tonight her line wasn't busy.

"Hello!" she said.

She sounded glad to hear from me, like the Diana of old. Static from somewhere drowned out my reply.

"Devin, is that you?" she asked.

"No. It's Garth. Who's Devin?"

Her voice fell. "A friend."

"I've heard that one before." I'd intended to keep this light, but at the moment wasn't having much luck. The truth, which I'd been avoiding, was no longer avoidable. She was seeing someone else, someone who rated a happier hello than I did.

"Well, now you know," she said.

"I guess I've known for some time now. I just didn't want to admit it."

"Neither did I, not even to myself, but especially not to you."

"Does that mean you won't be coming home for Christmas?"

"I'm not sure yet what it means."

"I would like to see you. If nothing else, to give you your present." One I hadn't bought yet.

"I'm sorry, Garth. I can't promise anything right now."

"I'm not asking for promises. I never have."

"I know that. I'm sorry."

"What is there to be sorry about? It's Christmas, isn't it? Fa, la la, la la . . . la la . . . la . . . la."

"Garth, please. . . . This isn't getting us anywhere."

"What the hell do you want me to do then? It's you who's feeling guilty, not me."

"But you're the one who called."

"Do you want me to hang up?"

"That might be best. Yes."

I didn't have to be told a second time. I hung up. I also hung around the phone for an hour, thinking she'd call back. When she didn't, I sat down in front of the fire and watched it burn out.

6

I was up and gone the next morning before Ruth's feet ever hit the floor. I went to my office, sat at my desk, and watched the sun rise. Cold, calm, and blue, the morning promised another beautiful day. But I didn't believe it. Not in my present state of mind.

The phone rang. I waited, hoping it would ring itself out. It didn't. On the sixth ring, I answered it. "Ryland here."

"Baldwin here," Diana said. "I'm sorry about last night. You took me by surprise. It has been a while."

"Not because I haven't tried. Your phone's been busy lately."

"I know it has."

"Would you rather I didn't call from now on?"

"For the time being perhaps. Why don't I call you?"

"You never do."

"I did today."

"I guess you did at that." I could see myself in the window. I wondered if I sounded as bad as I looked. "Is there anything else you wanted to say?"

"There are a lot of things I want to say. But now is not the time."

"When the time comes, let me know."

There was a pause before she said, "Well, I guess that's it then. Merry Christmas if I don't see you again."

"Same here."

I hung up and sat staring out the window, watching the morning unfold. Wisps of white now showed in the blue, and the sun was lightly veiled with clouds. I knew it was too good to last.

At home Ruth dried her hands on her robe and retrieved a sack from the back room. "Here," she said, handing it to me. "This is ready to go."

"What's in it?"

"Ham sandwiches, an apple, a fried fruit pie, a bottle of pop, and a few other things she might need."

"I should eat so well."

"You do." She went back to washing dishes while I poured myself a glass of juice. "You left early this morning," she said.

"I know."

"Anything wrong?"

"Diana doesn't think she's coming home for Christmas."

"I see."

"I wish I did."

"You want to talk about it?"

"Maybe later. Thanks, Ruth."

"You heading for the farm?"

"Eventually. I want to stop by and see how Will's doing."

"Tell him hello from me."

"I'll do that."

Before I left, I took my camera and case from the shelf in the hall closet. Even when Ruth wasn't trying, she didn't miss much.

"What's that for?" she asked.

"Mary. I thought a photograph might help identify her."

"And I thought she wouldn't let you get that close."

"She won't. But you never know."

The night before I'd put the battery charger on Jessie when I came into the house. She must have liked the extra attention because she started on the first try.

On the way to Fair Haven I noticed the sky had darkened to grey and only the sun's face shone through. Appropriate. Now the sky matched my mood.

Will Cripe stumbled down the steps of Fair Haven Church, righted himself, and hobbled across the churchyard toward the road. It had been years since I'd seen him move that fast. If his legs could have stood it, he would have been running. I stopped just in time to intercept him.

"Did you see her?" he asked.

"See whom?"

"Annie!"

"Annie who?"

He didn't answer.

"Why don't you tell me what's going on?" I asked.

"There's no time! Get out and help me find her!"

"Which way did she go?"

"I don't know. You take the cemetery and I'll look across the road." He was already on his way.

"Just remember to stay out of Willoby's Slough!" I shouted. But he ignored me.

I made a quick trip through the cemetery and came back to the church. When Will didn't appear, I went after him. Like Lucky two days before, he'd fallen on the ice of Willoby's Slough and couldn't get up.

"Anything broken?" I asked as I helped him to his feet.

"Just my pride." There were tears in his eyes. "Damn this disease! Won't it ever let up?" He walked away to stand by himself. When he returned, his eyes had cleared. "I'm sorry, Garth. That was uncalled for."

"I think you had every right."

He shook his head. "No. That's the one thing I vowed I'd never do, feel sorry for myself. It only makes it worse." He bit his lip to keep back the tears. "It's just that sometimes, like today, I wish I were a man again."

"And I wish I could be the man you are."

He put his hand on my shoulder. "Don't, Garth. I don't need your charity."

"I meant it. You know I've always admired you."

He smiled. There was wisdom in it. "You used to admire me. But you've grown up since then."

63

With nothing more to say, we walked up the hill together.

"I take it you didn't find her," Will said at the top.

"No. Did you?" We had been sheltered from the wind down in the slough. There on top of the hill I felt its cutting edge. Will, however, seemed not to notice.

"No. I'm sorry to say."

"Who *is* Annie?" I asked, for my sake as much as his.

"You remember the one I told you about, the one who loved Willoby's Slough? She's Annie." He brightened whenever he spoke of her.

"Annie who?"

"I'm tired, Garth. Will you give me a ride home?"

"That's your answer?"

"For now. Later we'll see."

"Answer me this. Did you see her?"

His face was radiant, the way it used to be when he'd gaze upon his day's work. "Yes. I saw her."

"You're sure it's Annie?"

"I'd bet my life on it."

At that moment the sun went under the clouds for good, and the chill wind seemed to take a bite of my heart. "I'd rather you wouldn't," I said.

"It's my life, Garth. Don't forget that."

I let Will off at his house, then drove to the farm. When almost there, I noticed a string of smoke rising from somewhere on Hoover's Ridge. Then it bent, like the wick of a candle, under the lowering clouds. I hung my camera on my shoulder and took the sack of food into the barn.

"Mary, you in here?"

The flutter of pigeons answered me.

I searched the barn from top to bottom, but didn't find Mary. I did find where she'd been sleeping in the hayloft, along with one of the blankets I'd brought her. The foil, paper towels, and toilet paper were there, too, but the axe, matches, and extra blanket had disappeared. Remembering the smoke I'd seen rising from Hoover's Ridge, I thought I knew where they'd gone.

The clouds continued to thicken around the sun, chilling

and darkening the day. When I entered the woods of Hoover's Ridge, it darkened even more, like shutters had been pulled shut. Opening my camera case, I took out a flash cube and inserted it. It sounded bulletlike as it snapped into place.

I came to the abandoned house and waited a moment to see who was home. Looking through a cracked window, I could see a fire burning on the hearth. It seemed to ask me in.

The extra blanket I'd given to Mary lay on the black leather chair. The box of matches sat on the floor to the right of the fireplace; the axe stood next to it. She hadn't moved out of the barn entirely, just enough to put her closer to Fair Haven.

That bothered me. The thought she might be sharing the house with the man who killed Lucky bothered me even more. I decided to wait for her, to try to warn her of her danger.

Pulling up the chair, I sat with my feet on the hearth, watching the fire. It purred and tugged at me, drawing me closer as it fell. I grew sleepy, fought it momentarily, then gave in to the fire. But I didn't sleep well. A two-headed dog haunted my dreams.

I awakened with a start. The fire had died and the house had gone cold. I could hear the wind whisk the leaves and a nearby tree moan. It took me a moment to realize where I was.

Then I realized something else. I wasn't alone. Someone stood at the door behind me, breathing softly, so as not to be heard. It drove the chill of the house into my bones.

"Mary, is that you?" I asked.

There was no answer.

Slowly I turned around to see who it was. No one was there. I got up and looked out the east window, but saw no one leaving.

Maybe I'd just imagined it. That sometimes happens when coming out of sleep. The monster beside your bed turns out to be your chest of drawers.

The room beyond, once a passageway, was the darkest one in the house. I approached it with caution, wanting to give my eyes time to adjust before I entered it.

As I stepped over the threshold, the timber came down at me without warning. It caught me on the right shoulder, slamming me against the door frame and knocking some splinters loose. Stunned, I fell to the floor, rolled over, and covered up. A second timber crashed to the floor where I had been an instant before. Drawing myself even tighter, my muscles coiled to take the blow, I waited for the third timber to fall. It never did. Apparently out of ammunition, my assailant had left.

I tried to rise, succeeded, then fell back down. My whole right side was numb and wouldn't listen to what I was trying to tell it. A few minutes later I tried again and managed to stay up.

Then I began counting parts to see if I was all there. Inching my right arm higher one painful hitch at a time, I finally raised it over my head. Maybe my collarbone wasn't broken after all. But I had a hard time convincing it of that.

Next I checked my camera to see how it looked. Nothing broken that I could see. But I'd know for sure when I developed my next roll of film.

I went outside, where it had started to snow. It gave the woods an eerie, fog-bound look as it closed in like dusk. Hard to believe it was still morning.

Beulah Peters' white Cadillac left Fair Haven Church just as I arrived. It turned south on Fair Haven Road and sped toward Oakalla, spinning its tires as it went. Though I shielded my eyes, I couldn't see who was in it because of the snow.

I wondered what Beulah was doing at the church. Like a lot of us, she had regular rounds and morning wasn't a time when I would have expected her at Fair Haven. Also, unless she was trying to beat the snow, why was she in such a hurry to leave?

Coop's purple De Soto was parked at the church. Maybe he could tell me. Maybe he would also drive me back to the farm to get Jessie. My right shoulder had started to throb, and my legs felt rubbery, unsure of themselves.

But when I got to Coop's office, someone had strewn his books from one end of it to the other. Coop sat at his desk with his head down in defeat, only the white puff of his hair showing, like an old dandelion gone to seed.

"Coop, what happened?"

He raised up to look at me, but never had a chance to answer.

> *I come to the garden alone,*
> *While the dew is still on the roses,*
> *And the voice I hear, falling on my ear,*
> *The Son of God discloses.*

Her voice was strong and clear, like a mountain chime. Its pure sweet song filled Fair Haven Church, swelled against its narrowed walls, and threatened to tear it apart at the seams.

> *And He walks with me, and He talks with me,*
> *And He tells me I am His own,*
> *And the joy we share as we tarry there,*
> *None other has ever known.*

When she finished, every nerve of my being was tingling. My cheeks were wet. I couldn't swallow the lump in my throat. That had been Grandmother's favorite song, hummed by her countless times as she sewed, then sung by Beulah Peters at Grandmother's funeral. Beulah had a fine contralto voice. Rich and deep, it boomed as she sang, made you sit up and take notice of it. And in her own way she had done Grandmother justice.

But Beulah's voice, as rich and fine as it was, couldn't compare to Mary's. I'd never heard such a beautiful voice, one so unpretentious, so pure in its tone, filled, as it were, with so much joy. I could almost see Grandmother Ryland sit back in her rocker and smile.

I turned to look at Coop. His face had gone as white as his hair.

"I know that voice," he said. "There is none other like it."

"From where?"

"Kentucky. My home."

"Whom does it belong to?"

"Annie. Annie Pate. At least that used to be her name." He looked skyward as tears welled up in his eyes. At that moment he

67

was the most reverend I'd ever seen him. "God, be praised!" he shouted. "I thought I would never hear her sweet voice again!" He smiled at me. "Don't you see, Garth. There's my answer. God has just spoken."

I didn't know what to say, so I kept my peace. He seemed so happy I was afraid to challenge him.

Instead I said, "Annie Pate. What can you tell me about her?"

His face darkened. The moment was over. I should have kept quiet. "I married her to Satan's apostle. That is my cross, and that's all you need to know."

"Coop, it's important I find out."

"No more important than my silence. That's all I'll say, Garth. Don't ask me more." He seemed to resent my asking as much as I resented his not answering.

"Why?" I persisted. "Why won't you tell me?"

"Something I fear."

"What do you fear? Is Annie in danger?"

"No, Garth. I fear Annie *is* the danger."

"What do you mean, 'Annie is the danger?'" A moment before he had been singing her praises. I wondered what had occurred to him to change his mind.

He shook his head. He wouldn't answer.

I followed him out to the De Soto. He left his office in the mess I'd found it. He made no attempt to locate Mary, or Annie, whichever her name was. If she meant as much to him as she seemed to, I wondered why he didn't pursue her. Perhaps, despite what he professed, he really didn't believe in miracles.

"Coop, what happened to your office?"

"I'm sorry. What was your question?"

"What happened to your office? Who threw your books all over the place?"

"I don't know." He gave me a helpless look, "I found it that way when I arrived at the church."

"When was that?"

"A few minutes before you, I think. Though it could have been longer."

"Did you happen to see Beulah Peters here at the church?"

"No. Not that I recall. Though she wouldn't have come had I been here. The same is true for me."

"Both of you are trying to do God's work," I pointed out. "You might try to get along with each other."

"No," he corrected. "I'm trying to do God's work. Beulah Peters is trying to do Beulah's work, which is not the same. Good day, Garth."

Once Mary began to sing, I'd forgotten how tired and sore I was. My legs reminded me on my way back into the church. After creeping up the basement steps to the vestibule, I double-checked my camera to make sure it was working. Then I waited.

Even at that I nearly missed her. She climbed down the ladder of the bell tower so quietly and quickly that she reached the door of the sanctuary before I could react.

"Mary!"

She turned to face me. As she did, I took her photograph, then hurriedly snapped two more. I wasn't prepared for what happened next. I thought she'd dart through the sanctuary door and leave. Instead, she charged me, going straight for the camera.

When I wouldn't let her have it, she began to pummel me with her fists. I ducked away, trying to protect myself and the camera. But she wouldn't let up. Soon she began to hit where the timber had caught me.

More from pain than in anger, I swept out with my left arm, trying to push her away. I pushed harder than I intended to and she went flying across the vestibule, cracking her head on the sanctuary door. I'll never forget the look of awakening that came over her face. She was in another time, another place, recalling a terrible memory. Then her look turned to me. It, too, was one I will never forget. It said I had done more than hurt her. I had betrayed her deepest trust.

"Mary, I'm sorry," I said, taking a step toward her.

But it was way too late for that. Backing away, as from the visage of Death himself, she regained her feet, and left an instant later.

7

I stopped at home long enough to unload my camera, put the roll of film in my pocket, and leave the picnic basket on the kitchen table. Ruth wasn't there, which was too bad. I needed to talk. From there I went to the drugstore to leave the roll of film. Spencer Davis, the owner, was busy with a customer.

So while I waited, I took a stroll around the drugstore. It, along with my office, was my refuge. Whenever things got too much for me, I'd duck in there, drink a lemon Coke with Spencer, and commiserate about the good old days. We never resolved anything, but I always felt better when I left. And it helped to know someone else remembered the S and B and the BAB, the Nickelplate and the Big Four, men with names like Fatty, Gravy, Tweeter, and Runt.

I handed Spencer the roll of film. "How soon can you have this for me?" I asked.

"By Thursday at the earliest."

"No earlier?" I was disappointed. Without her even knowing it, time might be running out on Mary.

"Nope. That's the best I can do," Spencer said.

"What time Thursday?"

"Check with me first thing in the morning. He's usually here then."

"I'll do that. Thanks."

Spencer looked disappointed. He thought I was there to

talk. Looking outside at the snow falling down, it seemed the perfect time.

"You haven't been in lately," he said.

"Something I plan to remedy soon."

"I'll be counting on it."

The name Annie had been spoken with love by three different men within the past two days. Paul Peters said it first, then Will, then Coop. Paul had fallen down the basement steps of Fair Haven Church; Will's dog Lucky had been killed; Coop had received a threatening letter, then his office ransacked. I doubted that was a coincidence. I went to see Paul at his home.

Paul and Beulah Peters lived in a big blue house on the west side of town. The house had a red roof, a brick porch and chimney, and a bay window that looked out on Elm Street. Strung to every bush and trellis, hung in every door and window, its Christmas decorations were vintage Beulah Peters, the way they loudly drew attention to themselves. And like Beulah, they seemed impervious to time, taste, and the elements.

From the porch I could hear Paul playing his piano. Though I didn't recognize the tune, I recognized the mood. It was one of building anger. Played by a symphony, it would end with the crash of cymbals.

I knocked on the front door. When no one answered, I knocked again. Looking through its oval glass, I saw Beulah Peters marching down the hall toward me. Her fur coat, Cossack's hat, and five-buckle overshoes said she was on her way out.

"Come in, Bart!" she boomed. "I was just leaving!"

"Lucky for me I'm here to see Paul."

Though I'd known her ever since I moved to Oakalla, she had never once called me Garth. It was either Bart or Charles or whatever came to mind. Perhaps it was unintentional. She wasn't known for her attention to detail. But I noticed she never forgot how to carry a grudge.

"The maestro's hard at work," she went on. "Disturb him at your own risk."

"Where are you off to?"

72

"Feed for my birds. Poor little dears won't make it for long in this weather without it."

Her bird feeder, like the rest of her house, was strung with lights.

"Why didn't you pick it up this morning?"

"Because I wasn't out this morning. I never go out on Tuesday. It's my morning to write. Even Paul knows better than to disturb me."

"What are you writing?"

"My autobiography."

"It have a title?"

"*Beulah.*"

"Catchy."

Her frown reproached me. "Sarcasm doesn't become you, Bart. Now if you'll excuse me . . ."

"Then it wasn't your white Cadillac I saw leaving Fair Haven Church?"

"When was that?"

"Earlier this morning."

She scowled. She didn't even want to consider the possibility. "No. I can assure you it wasn't." Then she charged past me and left.

I stamped the snow off my feet and went into the parlor. Paul sat in the center of the parlor playing his Baldwin grand piano. Facing him was a blue tile fireplace with an ebony mantle. Behind him white-curtained French doors led out onto a brick patio. In one corner hung a giant fern. A porcelain umbrella stand filled another corner. The walls were white, the floor black. An ashtray filled with cigarette butts sat on the piano bench beside Paul.

Paul continued playing, as the notes grew harsher. His delicate fingers struck the keys with incredible power. When he finished, he sat perfectly still for a moment with his hands flat on the keyboard, then leaned back, lighted a cigarette, and watched it burn.

"What is its title?" I asked.

"'Redemption.'"

73

"By?"

"Paul Peters. It's an original composition."

"It's very powerful."

"Is it? I hadn't noticed." Then he turned around, seeing me for the first time. "Did the storm blow out?" he asked.

"She left a few minutes ago. For bird seed."

"She has a basement full of it."

"Maybe she needed out of the house."

"Maybe she did. Mother has never approved of my playing. Probably because it's the one thing in my life she can't control." He looked at his hands. "Unfortunately, neither can I control it. The notes come whether I ask them to or not."

"Then why try to control it?"

"Why indeed." Then he smiled as the moment passed. He was back on familiar ground. "So, what brings you here? It's a first, I believe."

"Annie Lawson."

"What about her?"

"You mentioned her yesterday. I wondered why. Have you seen her lately?"

Though he tried to be casual, I noticed his hands trembled. "No. Have you?"

"Yes. I think I have."

"In Oakalla?"

"Yes. In Oakalla."

The news stunned him. I'd never seen Paul Peters at a loss for words before.

"What proof do you have?" he asked.

"A photograph, though it's not ready yet. I took it myself."

"Where? When?" He couldn't ask fast enough.

"That's all I'll say for now. Annie, if that's who it is, has been through some hard times. The last thing she needs is a lot of company." That was partly true. But if I took a hard look at myself, there was more to it than that.

"What kind of hard times?"

"A three year stay at Central State. Eight years without speaking so much as her name. Those kind of hard times."

"Before I tell you anything, I want to see her for myself."

"You can't, Paul. Take my word on it. She won't let you. Even if she would, I wouldn't let you. Her balance is too delicate."

"You want her for yourself, is that it?"

"Paul, be reasonable," I said. But he was closer to the truth than he knew.

"I can't, Garth. Not where Annie is concerned."

"You were in love with her?"

"Isn't that obvious?"

"Were you her lover?" I had to ask.

"No!" He leaped to his feet. "She wouldn't . . . She was married. To the world's most complete *bastard*."

"Why was he a bastard?" I remembered Coop had described him as Satan's apostle. That is if Annie Pate and Annie Lawson were one and the same.

"For the way he treated Annie. Like dirt, and worse. Some of the things he did to her . . . I tell you, Garth, it was all I could do to keep from killing the man."

"What was his name?"

"Charles Lawson. *Reverend* Charles Lawson, if you can believe that."

"He was a minister?"

"He was a preacher. He ministered very little."

"Where?"

"Fair Haven Church."

It was my turn to be stunned. Paul saw it on my face and asked, "What's wrong?"

"Nothing. Is Charles Lawson still around?" I remembered with dread all that had happened in and about Fair Haven Church recently, and that Annie had been moving ever closer to there.

"No. He left eight years ago. He and Annie both. In the middle of the night and without a goodbye. I haven't heard from either one of them since."

"Describe Annie for me," I said.

75

He shook his head. "I don't even want to try. She defied description."

"Long brown hair, warm brown eyes, a sweet soft voice?" I asked.

"On the contrary," he said, obviously pleased I'd missed the mark. "She had short blond hair, blue eyes, and a voice that could swell your heart and raise the roof at the same time. But that doesn't begin to describe her."

"Then she could sing?"

He laughed at my ignorance. "If you had ever heard her, you'd know not to ask that question. No one could sing like Annie." He took a long drag on his cigarette, letting the smoke leak slowly from his mouth. "No one," he repeated softly.

"What about her husband? What did he look like?"

"Like he got lost in the fifties and never found his way out again. Slick black hair, thin black mustache. About my height, I believe, but a bigger build. Cold unfriendly eyes. About the coldest I've ever seen. And a scar," he used the hand holding the cigarette to show me, "that ran from here to here." He traced a line from the corner of his right eye down to his chin.

"I don't recall ever meeting him."

"Believe me, Garth, once you met him, you'd never forget him."

"And you say he was a bastard?"

"A *complete* bastard."

"Then what did Annie see in him? More to the point, why did she stay with him?"

"I think she was afraid to leave him, afraid of what he might do to her. But to give the devil his due, he also had a power, an aura about him. When he stood up in the pulpit and spoke, you listened whether you wanted to or not. And he was a master at reaching those dark places in your soul you thought were safely hidden. He knew evil, Garth, and he knew it well. I'll give him credit for that."

"He sounds a little like Coop lately," I said.

Paul laughed. "That buffoon! He's all hot air. He wouldn't know evil if it were staring him in the face."

I let that pass. Paul, like his mother, had his differences with Coop.

"Did Annie have any other friends at the church?" I asked. I was thinking of Will Cripe in particular.

"Annie had all of the friends in the world. I don't know anyone who didn't like her."

"Special friends, then?"

"What exactly do you mean, Garth?"

"Was she seeing anyone else besides her husband?"

"You mean an affair?" He hated me for even asking.

"Believe me, Paul. I don't like that question any better than you do."

"Then why ask it?"

"Because I think Annie might be in danger."

He stiffened with resolve. "From whom?" he demanded. "In danger from whom?"

"I don't know, Paul. Maybe Charles Lawson. You haven't seen him here in Oakalla lately, have you?"

He looked away, his eyes avoiding mine. "No. I haven't."

"And your fall down the basement steps at Fair Haven Church—it was an accident, right?"

He turned back to me. "Who said it wasn't?"

"No one. I was just asking."

"Of course it was an accident." But he didn't want to talk about it. "Now if you'll excuse me. It's time to torture myself again."

"And your mother was right when she said it wasn't her white Cadillac out at Fair Haven Church this morning?"

He stared at the piano, his face self-mocking. "When have you known Mother to ever be wrong."

He buried his cigarette in the ashtray, then began to play. I recognized this tune. Too well. It was "MacArthur Park."

8

I spent the rest of the afternoon at my desk trying to write, but I still wasn't in the mood. The sky was low and grey, my whole right side was sore, and I kept thinking about Annie. I wanted her safe, preferably where I could keep an eye on her. My arms seemed ideal.

Snow blew down my neck all the way home. When I got there, I saw a light in the kitchen and gave silent thanks. After a day in the trenches, when even my shadow ached, nothing looked so good to me as a light in the house. I took off my coat and cap and sat down at the kitchen table.

"What's the matter?" Ruth asked. "You look like you lost your last friend."

"Something like that."

"Well, this should cheer you up."

She handed me a pencil drawing of myself. I took it, intending to lay it down on the table, but it never left my hands. Whoever had done the drawing had captured the essence of me, at least the way I always wanted to be seen. I knew only one person who knew me that well.

"Diana?" I asked.

"No. I found it in the bottom of the picnic basket."

It took a moment for that to register. When it did, I felt perfect for the first time in my life—a perfect idiot.

Still holding the drawing, I leaned back in my chair and sighed, "Ruth what have I done?"

"You name it. I can vouch for most of it."

"I mean to Annie. I shoved her today, broke all the trust between us."

"Who's Annie?"

"Annie is Mary's real name, Annie Lawson. She lived in Oakalla around eight years ago. I thought you might know her." Since she knew everything else about Oakalla, past and present.

Ruth shut off the stove and sat down at the table. She looked sad, unusual for her. "No, I don't know her. Karl died then, eight years ago, and that year and the next escape me completely. So why don't you start at the beginning."

So I started at the beginning and told her how my day had gone. In the telling, I began to understand why I shoved Annie, but that still didn't excuse it. Another time, another place, even under the same set of circumstances, it would never have happened. I'd have simply turned and walked away.

"What's done is done," she said when I finished. "You can't undo the harm, so don't even try."

"I know that. I just don't know where to go from here. At first I thought it was just a matter of finding out who she was. But after all that's happened I'm sure she's in danger. Whoever hit me with that timber wasn't playing games. He intended to hurt me."

"She might be the danger, too. Don't forget that."

"No. I know her too well."

She reached over, took the drawing from me, and studied it a moment. "You don't know her at all, Garth. Anybody who can see through you like that in one day, which took me all of five years, can do just about anything she puts her mind to."

"Even murder?"

"Even murder." She gave me a hard look. "You didn't say anything about that."

"I said whoever attacked me intended to hurt me. I assumed you understood."

"That puts a whole new light on things."

"Or a whole new shadow. Or as Frost said, the 'design of darkness to appall.'"

"Meaning?" She got up and began to set the table for supper. She thought best when she was on the move.

"He was wondering if there really is a conscious evil at work in the universe. Satan's work, as Coop called it."

"What did Frost decide?" she asked, setting my plate in front of me. Mine was yellow, hers red.

"He decided that he didn't know. He was just raising the question, that's all. Like me."

"Which I'm supposed to answer?" I got the blue coffee cup. She got the green one.

"You said you've lived longer than I have. That means you must be smarter."

"It means I'm smart enough not to waste my time trying to answer unanswerable questions. But I will say this. If Satan lives in Oakalla, I haven't met him yet."

"What about God?"

"Him either. But I've talked to Him long distance a time or two." She started to set some silverware down, then saw the water spots and looked at me. I raised my arms in surrender. Guilty as charged.

"What did He say?"

"Keep the line open."

"Have you?"

"I have. When you get to be my age, you try to keep all the options you can."

"So on the balance do you think life is good?"

"On the balance I think life is life. Knowing it's one or the other doesn't make it any easier to live. Only the people who care for you do that. Of course, they can make it harder, too. But only if you let them."

"Thanks, Ruth." I got up and put on my coat and cap.

"Where do you think you're going?"

"To visit an old friend. The day's not over. Maybe I can still do some caring."

"What about supper?"

"I should be home in time. If not, stick mine in the oven."

"Where have I heard that before?"

I drove to Will Cripe's and parked in his drive. The Alberta clipper that had brought the sudden snow had just as quickly moved on. A few flakes fell from a low sky, but there was an orange tint to the clouds and a slice of blue in the west. Standing in Will's drive, I watched dusk gather around Fair Haven Church and wondered about Annie, where she'd be sleeping that night. Then I went inside.

Will had a fire going. He also had a glass of brandy in his hand and a drowsy look on his face, like he was at peace with himself and his world. I was tempted to turn around and leave. Whatever communion he was holding it wasn't with me in mind.

"Who is it?" he asked.

"Garth Ryland."

"Don't you ever knock?"

"I didn't want you to get up." I walked into the room where he could see me. "Were you expecting someone else?"

"No. No one else," he said. Though his eyes said differently.

"I can come back later."

"No. Not later. As long as you're here, you might as well stay. The bottle's here by my chair. You know where the glasses are."

I went into the kitchen and got myself a glass. As I did, I noticed the dirty dishes in the sink were gone, also the pots and pans on the stove. I turned on the light to make sure. The kitchen looked ten times cleaner than yesterday.

I went back into the living room, poured myself half a glass of brandy, and sat down on the hearth. The fire at my back felt good.

"You hire yourself a maid?" I asked.

"How's that?"

"The kitchen. Somebody cleaned it."

He smiled. "I know." But that's all he would say.

We sat for a while without speaking or feeling the need to speak, the way only old friends can do. On the wall behind Will hung a metal Berger Beer sign showing two pointers on point.

Across the room was an oak-framed print of a fisherman standing in a boat in the middle of a lake. His arm cocked and at the ready, he was about to start his forward cast.

I'd wanted the sign and the print since the day I saw them. Partly because they belonged to Will, and I knew their history. Partly because each captured the same tense moment of anticipation and the reason why I hunted and fished. But the main reason was the memories they evoked, and the people who'd made those memories with me.

"Why are you here, Garth?" Will finally asked. "Is it just to pass the time?"

"Yes and no. I'm here to see you, drink your brandy, and sit by your fire. But I'm also here because of Annie Lawson."

"Who have you been talking to?"

"Paul Peters."

"What did he have to say?"

I told him all that Paul had told me.

"He didn't lie, Garth," Will said when I finished. "That's about the way it was."

"Annie's husband was as bad as Paul said he was?"

"Worse, Garth. In all of my years he's the only man I've ever truly hated. The way he treated Annie was a crime. I begged her to leave him, but she wouldn't."

"Did he physically abuse her?"

"I never saw the bruises, nothing I could prove anyway. It was just the way he treated her in general. With contempt, like he did everything else."

"Maybe she encouraged it."

"And maybe you don't know what you're talking about either."

"Then why did she stay with him?"

"She was twenty years old. Where was she to go? What was she to do? She was five hundred miles away from home with no education, and married to a man she'd loved since she was twelve. If you had been her, what would you have done?"

"Probably shot the sonofabitch."

The look on Will's face said that was a possibility.

"Do you think that's what happened?" I asked.

"At this point in my life I don't want to guess. What good would it do anyway?"

"It might explain why she came back here."

He smiled. "How do you know she's come back here?"

"Hasn't she?"

His smile deepened and his eyes shone. "Yes."

"To your house?"

"Yes again."

"How do you know?"

"Before when she was here and I was away building, I'd let things slide here at home. I'd say I'd do it tomorrow, and you know how that goes, tomorrow never came. Then I'd get so tired of looking at the mess I'd hate to come home at night because it gave me a guilty conscience, and I knew without thinking twice about it my mother was rolling over in her grave. If there was anything my mother hated, it was a mess." He picked up his glass and took a drink of brandy. "But sometimes, not always and not so I could ever predict it, I'd come home and find the house clean from top to bottom." He smiled at me. "Annie's work. Though when I'd see her next and thank her, she'd just smile and let it go at that."

"Like now," I said, starting to understand.

"Like now. When I came back this morning, I found the house clean as new."

"Have you talked to her?"

He shook his head. "No."

"Do you think you can?"

"If anyone can."

"She's not the same Annie you remember. Three of the past eight years she spent in Central State. The last five in Four Corners. During that whole time she didn't speak at all."

"It doesn't matter. She used to stutter and that frustrated her, so she never did talk all that much anyway. But we always understood each other."

I felt a knot in my chest. "You were lovers?"

"We loved the same things, Garth—the outdoors, morning

84

quiet and evening dew, long walks and to be alone. So yes, you could say we were lovers."

"Sorry. But I had to ask."

His smile was gentle and forgiving. "I know. For both our sakes. And you'll keep overturning every obstacle until you get next to her. But it won't get you anywhere with Annie. She'll never let you get that close."

"How did you get that close?"

"By not trying. Something you don't know how to do."

"So what do you suggest?"

"Stay away from around here for the next day or so. Give me a chance to talk to her."

The knot in my chest began to swell. "I'm not sure I can do that, Will. I think Annie's in danger. In fact, I'm almost sure of it."

"She is in danger," he said quietly. "But you're not helping any."

"And you think you can do better?"

He straightened, his jaw set, his eyes certain, the way I first remembered him. "Yes, I think I can do better."

"You're the boss." I answered as I once did whenever he'd put me in my place. Then I stood and offered my hand. "Take care of yourself."

Though no longer calloused, his hand was still firm and dry. It felt good in mine.

"You do the same," he said. His face hardened as he added, "One more thing, Garth. If one of these nights I do happen to die before I wake, I want you to remember something. We are what we are. A leopard can't change his spots no matter how hard he tries. Snow leopard or black panther, he's one and the same inside the skin."

"Meaning?"

"You're a smart man. If the time comes, you'll figure it out."

"You give me too much credit."

"No more than you deserve."

I got in Jessie and drove home. I should have stayed longer, would have stayed had I known. It was the last time I ever saw Will Cripe alive.

9

I walked to work the next morning with Will Cripe on my mind. I knew he had the heart, but I wondered if he had the strength to look after both himself and Annie. Still, despite my fears, I owed him that chance.

The snow had left a powdery blanket that whitened the lawns and frosted the trees and bushes. Snow sparkles blew from the trees and dusted the streets. I had splotches in my hair and on the sleeves of my coat. Zipped inside my coat, right over my heart, I carried Annie's drawing of me.

At my office I struggled to remove my coat and cap. My right shoulder and arm had stiffened in the night and were almost too sore to move. And except to catch a baseball and dribble a basketball, I'd never asked much of my left hand, so it wasn't much help. Frustration was about to set in when I saw Karen Wilson standing outside my office door. For the moment she made me forget all about my sore shoulder.

Karen Wilson was tall and willowy with hazel eyes, honey-blond hair, and the loveliest legs in Oakalla. She was in her early thirties, married to Maynard Wilson, a respected lawyer in town, and a lawyer herself. Last spring she and I had become more than friends, but under extraordinary circumstances, and when they ended, so did we.

I hadn't seen her in six months. She used to run along Gas Line Road every morning, but that had stopped, too. I missed seeing her, especially on those mornings when I had a hard time getting going. For a heart starter, she was ten times better than a cup of coffee.

She carried in a paper plate wrapped with aluminum foil and set it on my desk.

"What's the occasion?"

"It's Christmas, or had you forgotten?"

"It must've slipped my mind."

"So how have you been?" she asked. "You look great!"

"So do you."

She did, too. Her cheeks were rosy from the cold and her face was all smiles. She wore a blue down vest over her yellow sweatsuit. I remembered she wore yellow a lot. It had become one of my favorite colors.

"Well, I'd better get going," she said.

"You running today?"

"I do every day I'm here in Oakalla."

"Then why haven't I seen you lately?"

Her smile faded. "I don't run Gas Line Road anymore. I run south instead."

"You get tired of dodging the chuckholes?"

"Yeah. In my heart."

"I know the feeling."

"It won't work, you know that," she said.

"What won't?"

"Us."

I didn't answer. I'd fought my own battles on the subject, and lost every one of them.

"Tell me I'm right," she said.

"About what?"

"Us. It won't work."

"You're right. It won't work."

"Say it like you mean it."

I stared at her yellow sweatsuit, the curve of her hips, the flow of her thighs. I knew what was beneath it. For starters, a whole lot of woman who was as interesting as she was lovely.

"It's hard, under the circumstances," I said.

88

"What are the circumstances?"

"You are the circumstances."

She nodded. She understood. "That's why I don't run Gas Line Road anymore. I knew if I saw you here I'd want to stop."

I smiled at her. "For what it's worth, I'm glad you did."

She smiled back. "For what it's worth, so am I." Then she noticed Annie's drawing of me on my desk. "What's that?" she asked.

"See for yourself. I brought it from home this morning to hang here. It's to help remind me who I am."

"When did you ever need reminding?"

"You'd be surprised."

She picked the drawing up and studied it. As she did, the smile left her face. "I'm jealous," she said, handing it back to me. "She knows you better than I do."

"How do you know it's by a woman?"

"Isn't it Diana's?"

"No. Someone else."

"Then I am jealous. Do I know her?"

"No. Neither do I. As you can see, I'm at a disadvantage."

"I might worry, Garth. Someone that . . ." she searched for the right word, "*wise*, could break your heart."

"So I've been told."

"Well, I'm off. Merry Christmas."

"You too."

She left. I walked to the window and watched her go. Nobody would ever look better running along Gas Line Road than Karen Wilson.

I sat down and opened the foil to see what she'd brought me. Peanut butter fudge. It was delicious. Grandmother Ryland couldn't have done better.

Then I set the fudge aside and began to type. Until Diana came home, if Diana came home, this was the best I was going to feel about Christmas.

I finished that afternoon. The following day I'd read it to see if it was any good, but while I was still in the mood, there was someplace I wanted to go.

Big Charlie's Country Store sat in the pines about fifty yards off of Wisconsin 13, just south of Friendship. Built of logs, it smelled like apple barrels and wood chips inside and was one of my favorite places to shop.

Big Charlie was a Chippewa Indian whose off-white hair matched the off-white T-shirt beneath his charcoal coveralls. He reminded me of Grandmother Ryland. His face had the same compassion, the same forbearance. He couldn't make much of a living out there. He was too far off the beaten track. Yet there he was and there he stayed because that's where he wanted to be. I had to like him for that.

"How long are you open?" I asked.

"How much money you have?"

"Not much."

"Just about to close then."

I smiled. He smiled back.

"What do you have in moccasins?" I asked.

"What do you want in moccasins?"

"Something large, fur-lined if possible."

"For you?"

"No. For my housekeeper. She's a big woman."

"How big?"

I held up my hand to show him Ruth's height. "Shoulders like this." I spread my hands apart. "She needs a new bathrobe, too, but she'd never wear whatever I bought."

He nodded. "I've got one like that, too."

"Housekeeper?"

"Wife. Sometimes housekeeper."

He showed me several pairs of moccasins. I liked them all but picked a russet pair lined with rabbit fur. I just hoped they fit.

"Anything else?" he asked when I set them on the counter.

"I'll look around."

I walked through the store, looking at jackets, ski vests, and sweaters. Diana would look good in any of them, especially the long black wool coat with the sable collar. I didn't know if it was in style, but I knew class when I saw it and it was certainly that. So was Diana. They would make a natural pair.

But I couldn't afford it. Even if I could, it was too much for this Christmas. She would read too much into it, and I'd have too much invested to feel comfortable giving it.

"Having any luck?" Big Charlie asked on my second trip around the store.

"Not much."

"Keep looking. You'll find something."

I nodded. For his sake and mine I'd try.

I finally did find something, a necklace made with Indian beads, quiet tones of ivory and blue. I liked its subtlety. Diana was flashy enough herself. She didn't need much decoration.

I carried the necklace to the counter. "This didn't come from Hong Kong, did it?" I asked.

"No. None of that stuff in here. You got my word on that."

"Do you know who made this necklace?"

He examined it, then smiled. "My wife did. The old way, the way her grandmother taught her."

"I'm glad somebody did." I looked in my wallet. I didn't have enough cash to pay for both the moccasins and the necklace. "Can you hold the necklace until tomorrow? I'm a little short of cash right now."

"You got a check?"

"I might have." I looked in my wallet and found a folded check that had been in there so long only the ink was holding it together. "I've got this," I said.

"That'll do."

When he added up what I owed him, I wrote the check and gave it to him. "Aren't you afraid it'll bounce?" I asked.

"Your credit's good," he said. "You've been in here before."

"That was at least two years ago."

"I still remember." He studied the necklace before he put it into a bag. "This for your woman?"

"It's for a woman. I'm not so sure she's mine anymore."

He held up the necklace and smiled. "Then this will win her back."

"You think so?"

"Maybe." His face grew solemn. "Worth a try at least."

91

I nodded and left.

On the way home I cut across country, ending up on Grandmother Ryland's road. It was a beautiful evening—white and still, stark contrasts of shadows and light, everything in full focus, like a Leo Gohler painting. It was too bad he only did barns. I would have loved to have seen his portrait of Annie Lawson.

I slowed, intending to stop at the farm to try to make my peace with her, but at the last minute decided against it. I'd promised Will Cripe I'd give him at least a day to try to talk to her. If I barged in now, I might ruin everything. But as I passed the farm, then turned at sunset onto Fair Haven Road, I began to feel uneasy, and though I continued on to Oakalla, to home, hearth, and friendship, the feeling never quite went away.

10

With no way around it and time growing short, I stopped at the Marathon to buy a Christmas tree from the Boy Scouts. The tree I chose must have had a tough life, but I figured if I didn't buy it no one would. I'd long ago given up trying to find the perfect Christmas tree. No sense in expecting more of it than I did of myself.

I drove home with a smile on my face. Knowing Ruth, she would zero in on the tree and never see the bag in my hand.

"Where did you get *that?*"

"Where did I get what?" With the tree blocking her view, I stuffed the bag carrying the gifts between some coats in the hall closet.

"That thing, whatever it is, you dragged in."

"At the Marathon."

"How much did it cost you?"

"Two dollars a foot. Why?"

"I hoped you'd stolen it. At least you'd have an excuse."

"I think it has character."

"So does poison ivy. But you won't see me paying two dollars a foot for it."

I stared at her through the tree. She stared back at me. I had her number. She had mine. After 6½ years there weren't too many secrets between us. "Where do you think we ought to put it?" I asked.

"How about in the fireplace?"

"Seriously."

"I am serious. Tiny Tim wouldn't have that tree."

"How about the southwest corner of the living room?"

She turned back to the stove. "Do as you like. If anybody asks, I had nothing to do with it."

"Do you remember where we put the stand?"

"It's somewhere in the basement."

The stand was in the basement, and the decorations were in the attic. But that must have made sense. That was the way we did it every year.

I made my rounds and soon had the tree up. Without realizing it, I'd started to whistle.

"How does it look?" I asked.

Ruth came into the living room. "Like someone shot it and left it for dead."

"I mean for level."

"It needs to go to the east."

"How far?"

"Boston would be just about right."

I ignored her and went about my task.

"Don't you know anything besides 'Jingle Bells'?" she asked.

"Christmas is coming, or didn't you hear?"

"I heard. I also remember the way you were last Christmas. You and Scrooge." Then she added, "Up until Diana came home."

"I promise this year will be different."

"I'll believe it when I see it."

"But you will help me decorate the tree?"

"When?"

"After supper."

She hesitated, then said, "I can't. I'm invited out."

"What about supper?" I noticed that even though she was in the kitchen, nothing was cooking.

"You're on your own tonight."

"You got a date?" I asked.

"I'm going bowling."

94

"By yourself?"

She bristled. "No. I told you I was invited out."

"He sounds like the last of the big spenders."

"You should talk. When was the last time you spent money on a woman?"

"Today, as a matter of fact."

"Not counting Christmas and birthdays."

"Seventy-six or seventy-seven, I forget which."

"That's what I thought."

I started for the stairs, but stopped before I turned the corner. "Are you going to tell me who he is or not?"

"You promise not to laugh?"

"I promise not to laugh."

"Willard Coates."

"Willard Coates! And he's spending money on you! Ruth, that's a first! The last time Willard opened his wallet a pterodactyl flew out!"

"I told you not to laugh."

"What did you promise him anyway?"

"I didn't promise him a thing. So get your mind out of the gutter. Which is where I'll be if I let myself listen to you."

"Sorry. It just struck me as funny, that's all."

I went upstairs to the attic after the decorations. While I was there, I opened some boxes I hadn't been into for years and played a few minutes of 'remember when'. Then I carried the decorations downstairs and set them beside the tree. Maybe I'd put them on later.

Ruth came into the living room wearing black slacks, a red blouse, shoes, and earrings. "How do I look?" she asked.

"Stunning. Willard won't be able to keep his hands off of you."

She just glared at me. "By the way," she said, "I put in a call to Kentucky. A friend of a friend of a friend might know someone who knows Annie's parents. Annie Pate, I believe you said her name was, before she got married."

"Where are they?"

"We can't be sure it's them yet. But there's this old couple

95

down in Harlan County, which is in southeastern Kentucky right on the Tennessee border, who had just this one daughter late in life. She married young and came north with her husband, and they haven't seen her since. That's been nearly ten years ago."

"And?" I could tell by the smile on her face there was more.

"Her name is Annie Pate. Her parents' names are Virgil and Rhodonna Pate. But we're still trying to make contact with them. We're not even sure they're still alive."

"It sounds like our Annie," I said.

"*Our* Annie?"

"It's just an expression. Keep after her parents, but if you reach them, don't tell them where Annie is yet. I don't want to get their hopes up. And while you're at it, see if you can find out where her husband went from here."

"Anything else?"

I smiled at her. "Have a good time tonight."

"I plan to."

A few minutes later Ruth left with Willard Coates. A few minutes after that I walked to the Corner Bar and Grill. Sniffy Smith sat at the bar, drinking a beer and eating his supper. I looked around the room. Seeing nowhere to hide, I decided to join him.

Sniffy Smith was my barber, who only cut hair on Fridays now that he was retired. Since his retirement he'd been a fixture at the Marathon, and ever since his controversial opinion on marijuana had appeared in the *Oakalla Reporter*, somewhat of a celebrity among his cronies. For me a half hour with Sniffy was like a half hour at a carnival, part adventure and part amusement, and usually long enough.

"I got a Christmas card from Joe Turner today," Sniffy said as I sat down.

Sniffy had taken Joe Turner under his wing ever since Joe's girlfriend, Frieda Whitlock, had been killed the past spring. He and I had looked after Joe until Joe decided in September that there were too many memories in Oakalla, and too much of the world he hadn't seen.

"Where is Joe now?" I asked.

"Back home in Tennessee. He'll probably stay there, he said."

"That's probably best."

Sniffy nodded, then looked down at his beer. "Best for him anyway. I'm going to miss him."

"That's the way of the world, or so I'm told. Some of us stay. Some of us go."

"Yeah, it's a kick in the nuts, ain't it," Sniffy said. "Especially around Christmas time."

I ordered a draft of Leinenkugels and sat drinking it while Sniffy finished his supper. Surrounded by smoke and silence, my earlier feeling of good will had started to slip away from me. Like all bars, the Corner Bar and Grill was a lonely place to be on a Wednesday night. As Sniffy said, especially around Christmas time.

"Were you at the Marathon yesterday?" I asked.

"From sun up to sun down. Why?"

"I just wondered if you saw Beulah Peters' white Cadillac go by yesterday morning?"

"I saw it go by once, heading north on Fair Haven Road."

"Did you happen to see who was driving it?"

"Nope. I never paid that much attention."

"But you didn't see it coming back?"

"Wasn't looking for it. Should I have been?"

"No. I thought I saw it out at Fair Haven. I just wanted to make sure."

The next time Hiram, the bartender, came by I ordered supper and another draft of Leinenkugels. Like me, Sniffy was in no hurry to get home, so I bought him another draft too.

"You heard Paul Peters fell down the basement steps at Fair Haven Church?" I said.

"I heard. I'm glad he didn't break those precious hands of his. Ruin that career he's always talked about and never had." He stopped to look at his own hands. "They were only good for cutting hair, but at least they were good for something."

"I take it you don't like Paul."

"I like him well enough. His mother, too, though God

97

knows why. But Paul's too much of a crybaby to suit me. Whenever I ask, he's always got an excuse for not playing that piano of his. He probably thinks all I like is honky-tonk. But hell, I like some of that long-hair stuff, too."

"I think Paul's reasons for not playing the piano might go deeper than that," I said. "I think there was someone he once loved who, when she left, took the heart of his music with her."

Sniffy sniffed loudly, the way he did whenever he disagreed with you. "And who might that be?"

"You probably don't know her. Her name was Annie Lawson."

Sniffy sniffed again, louder than before. It even got Hiram's attention. "Hell yes, I know her!" he said. "Tongue-tied as a rabbit, but about the prettiest little thing to ever pass through this town. Married to Simon Legree she was. Meanest Goddamn man I think I've ever met. And he looked the part."

"Paul said he had a scar on his cheek."

"Who's that?"

"Charles Lawson. Annie Lawson's husband."

"Damnedest scar you ever saw. It looked like he'd gotten it in a knife fight somewhere. Wouldn't surprise me a bit if he had."

"You ever hear him preach?"

"Once. That was enough for me. He had me damned to hell in so many ways I spent the next year cleaning out my closets, looking for all the demons I was sure were hiding there. No sir, Garth! Once was enough for me. If he couldn't save you from hell, he'd flat scare it out of you."

"It sounds like he wasn't all bad."

"Nobody is, I guess. But he comes about as close to it as anybody I've ever met."

"You haven't by chance seen him around lately, have you?"

"Here? In Oakalla?" He folded his arms and looked indignant. "What would he be doing back here?"

"That's what I'd like to know. But when I asked Paul Peters I got the impression Paul might have seen him. Will Cripe gave me the same impression, though neither came right out and said it. Then Coop . . ." I stopped. I'd promised not to tell anyone about the menacing letter he'd received.

"What about him?" Sniffy asked.

"Nothing. It's off the record."

"No. To answer your question. I haven't seen Charles Lawson around lately. I'd remember him if I had."

"What do you think happened to him?" I asked.

"How should I know? One day he was here, and the next day he wasn't. Her either, if I remember right. If I'd have been her, I'd have shot him." Sniffy blinked, owl-like, and looked wise. "Maybe that's what happened to him."

I looked at myself in the mirror and saw a man who knew better. "From what I understand, Annie wasn't the kind of person who would kill anyone."

"Pushed far enough, I'll bet she would. Just like you or I would. You can't tell from the outside what a person's thinking. Once I saw her get so mad at him the smoke was rolling from her ears. If she'd had a gun, I swear she would have shot him right there."

"Why was that?"

"I forget. It happened on the sidewalk right there in front of my barber shop. Since you mentioned Paul Peters, why don't you ask him. He was there at the time."

"When was this in relation to the time when the Lawsons left town?"

"Hell, Garth, I don't know. It must've been warm out. That's all I know. Otherwise, I wouldn't have had my door open to hear what was going on."

"Excuse me a moment, Sniffy."

I climbed down off my bar stool and made a phone call to Will Cripe. Without warning, something told me he was in danger.

Will, however, answered on the first ring.

"Will, this is Garth. Are you all right?"

"Why wouldn't I be?" His voice sounded sharp, the way it used to on those rare occasions when he ran out of patience with me.

"No reason. I was just checking."

"Did you forget our agreement?"

"No. I didn't forget. Have you had any luck with Annie?"

"No. But I'm working on that now. And I'd appreciate it if you'd let me do things my way."

"Sorry. My good intentions got in the way of my judgment."

His voice softened. "Usually a forgivable offense. Goodbye, Garth."

I broke the connection but didn't hang up for a while. Something in the way he said it sounded final.

"Something wrong?" Sniffy asked when I returned to my seat at the bar.

"A feeling I have. Nothing I can put my finger on."

"I sometimes get those myself. They usually don't amount to much."

"You're probably right." I took a drink of Leinenkugels and poked at my tossed salad with my fork. "I see Danny got Coop's car fixed," I said. "What was wrong with it?"

"Well, it wasn't the fuel pump like you thought it was. He had water in his gas."

"Where did he get that?"

"Hard to say. Danny thinks it was probably condensation, which you get this time of year when the weather turns cold. To complicate things, the man never puts in more than a dollar or two's worth of gas every time he stops. And to my knowledge he hasn't changed his oil since he's been here, which doesn't help any either. If he wasn't so damn cheap, it probably never would have happened." Sniffy took a drink of his beer and watched the bubbles flow. "You couldn't convince the preacher of that, though. He damn near called Danny a liar to his face."

"What did he think happened?"

"He was convinced somebody sneaked into his garage and poured the water into his tank."

I thought of the letter Coop had gotten, the fact that someone had wrecked his office. "He might have reason."

"How so?"

"I can't say, Sniffy. I promised I wouldn't."

100

"Well, in any case, the man might be a miser, but I think he learned his lesson. He came in this afternoon and filled his tank to the top. Said something to me about having to go up north tonight where he used to preach and lead a revival."

"It's a little cold for revivals, isn't it?" I asked.

"That's what I thought. But I'm sure that's what he said."

"Maybe he's got another reason for heading up north."

"Which is?"

"I don't know, Sniffy. I'll ask him the next time I see him."

"You think maybe somebody really is out to get the preacher?"

"It's a possibility," I said.

"I wonder why. He ain't the most popular act to ever hit this town, but I wouldn't put him in the same league as old Charles Lawson Legree. Now there was a man that needed got."

"Maybe he still does."

"What was that?"

"Nothing, Sniffy. Just a thought I had."

Sniffy finished his beer and left for the back room, where there was a euchre game starting up. I finished my supper and sat staring into the bar mirror, wondering where I went from here. I could either go home and sit around and feel sorry for myself, or I could go home and do something productive, like trim the Christmas tree. Or I could stay, drink another draft of Leinenkugels, and stare at myself in the mirror.

I went home. When I got there, I opened Jessie's trunk, took out Will's pick and shovel, and carried them down to the basement. Though my father once said I couldn't figure out the mechanism of a potato masher, through trial and error—mostly error—I had acquired some mechanical skills over the years and some tools as well.

Fixing a wire wheel to my electric grinder, I began to burn the rust off of Will's shovel. As the wheel whirled and the sparks flew in a gold stream, burnishing the steel of the shovel until it shone, I felt a real sense of accomplishment, one I had been reaching for but had not quite reached in my writing lately. I knew I needed more time like this, when nothing was at stake and the world went on without me. The trick was to find it.

The phone was ringing when I shut off the grinder. I ran upstairs to answer it, but by the time I got there, I heard only a dial tone. Quickly I dialed Will's number, then thought better of it and broke the connection before the dial could complete its last circuit. Still, I held the receiver in my hand, thinking that no matter what Will had said, I should go ahead and make the call. But I didn't.

11

The next morning I beat Ruth downstairs and put the coffee on. I'd puttered in the basement awhile longer, gone to bed early, heard Ruth come in and everything else that went on in the house for the next five hours, and finally fallen asleep sometime between four and six, just long enough to have a bad dream and wake up with a start. Diana had come back to Oakalla to stay and we'd gotten married in Fair Haven Church. I was the happiest man on earth until the morning after, when, lying in my arms, she turned out to be Beulah Peters.

Ruth came down the stairs hitting every step harder than the one before. I was afraid by the time she reached bottom she'd go through the floor.

"What happened to you?" I asked as she limped into the kitchen.

"I twisted my ankle."

"Badly?"

"It wasn't goodly, I can tell you that."

"How did you twist it?"

"In the parking lot of the bowling alley. I stepped on a bottle."

"Throwaway or returnable?"

She glared at me.

"What did Willard have to say about it?" I asked.

"Not much. He was too busy chasing the bottle down."

"It must've been a returnable."

She sat down at the table. "How did your night go?" she asked.

"It went."

Her brows rose. "I see. It wouldn't hurt, you know, for you to go out and have some fun once in a while."

"I hear you."

"Then why don't you do it?"

"There's no future in it."

"Why does there have to be a future in it? Willard and I went bowling for the first and last time."

"That's because he beat you," I said.

"How do you know that?"

"Well, didn't he?"

"Three straight games."

"But you had a handicap."

"What was that?"

"Your ankle."

"That didn't happen until we were on our way out."

I smiled. "You put money on the game, didn't you?"

"What do you think?"

"That was a mistake."

"I realized that later."

"How much later?"

"When he broke out his own ball, gloves, and shoes."

"How badly did he beat you?"

"Not bad, once I got over the shock."

"Don't worry about it. I once bet him he couldn't do fifty pushups. He was at seventy-five and counting when I left. He didn't even bother to take off his tie."

"Last night either," she said. "I think he sleeps in it."

"You mean you don't know?"

She got up and limped to the stove, poured us each a cup of coffee, then got the half-and-half from the refrigerator. "I'll pretend I didn't hear that," she said as she sat down.

"Which brings us back to me."

"Which brings us back to you."

"I don't know, Ruth. Every time I try to explain myself on the subject I don't do a very good job. I know I love Diana and I really miss her. I know she's sleeping with a guy named Devin and that hurts like hell. I know I should date other women, but I can't make myself. So what does that make me?"

"Don't ask me. I've been trying for 6½ years to answer that question. But I do know one thing. You'd like to think you're above temptation. But you're not. And that might have something to do with what happened between you and Karen Wilson this past summer. And . . ." she paused to make sure she drove her point home, "that might have something to do with what you're feeling for Annie now."

"How do you know what I feel for Annie?" Because I wasn't at all certain myself.

"I can see it in your eyes, hear it in your voice whenever her name comes up. A word to the wise, Garth. Try to keep your distance."

"I'm not sure I can where she's concerned."

"Then be prepared to suffer the consequences."

After breakfast I drove to Will Cripe's house. I couldn't wait any longer to find out what he'd learned from Annie. Will wasn't home. His back door stood wide open and there was a chill in the house.

I went into the living room where Will's afghan lay in a heap beside his chair. Everything seemed in place, like the last time I was there. Only Will was missing.

I felt something catch in my throat and cling there. The empty house brought back too many memories of Grandmother Ryland's, my first trip back there after she died. It seemed the heart, the life and love, had gone out of the place, never to return again.

I walked out the back door and down the hill to the edge of Willoby's Slough. Looking across the trackless snow, rose-colored in mirror of the dawn, I felt cold throughout. Lucky had been trailing Annie when he was killed. Will had disappeared on the same night he was supposed to meet with her. Either Ruth and Coop were right and she *was* the danger, or it stalked her so closely it had become her shadow.

Returning to the house, I saw a familiar car pull into the drive. It was Coop's purple De Soto. He'd just started to get out of the car when he saw me coming across the yard toward him.

"Don't go into the house," I said.

His look said he was going to challenge me. "Why not? Will sent for me."

"When?"

"Yesterday afternoon. He called and said he needed to see me. But I couldn't come. I was ready to leave for Ricelander at the time."

"Did he say what he wanted to see you about?"

"Only that it was personal, that's all."

"Nothing else?"

"No. Will is a quiet man. He usually keeps his own counsel. That's why I was surprised to hear from him, why I came at dawn this morning." His eyes were on mine. I was surprised at their power. "Has something happened to Will?" he asked.

"I don't know. Will was here last evening. He's not now. But since the dead tell no tales, you can draw your own conclusions."

He gave me a curious look. "Why would you say that?"

"A hunch, that's all. Blame it on Satan if you want."

"Don't joke about such things, Garth. I've seen Satan's work. I've seen into his heart and through his eyes. I know what he can do."

"As I'm starting to learn. Now if you'll excuse me, Coop, I have a phone call to make."

"Are you sure I can't be of some help?"

"Thanks, Coop. Not at the moment anyway."

He got into his De Soto and drove back toward town. I went into Will's house and called Clarkie.

"I'm at Will Cripe's, Clarkie. I need you here now."

"Why?"

"I'll tell you when you get here."

"What about the coroner, you need him?"

106

"No. Not yet."

While I waited for Clarkie, I took down the metal beer sign with the pointers on it, then the print of the fly fisherman. Will was dead. I didn't need to see his body to tell me that. Soon the scavengers would come, and I'd be damned if I'd let some third cousin have what was mine by right, or worse, learn too late he'd thrown them away with the rest of the trash. Will had promised them to me. The least I could do was keep that promise.

I picked up the afghan, folded it, and set it in Will's chair. When I looked down at the floor where it had been, I discovered something that took me by surprise. A .22 Colt target pistol lay on the floor under the edge of Will's chair. Twenty years ago, after a hard day of hammering and sawing, he and I had shot cans with it to relax.

I opened my billfold and took out a dollar bill. Using the rolled bill, I lifted the pistol by its trigger guard and examined it. It was tarnished, rust-stained, and thick with dust. I smelled the muzzle. It hadn't been fired recently.

"What's up?" Clarkie asked, tramping into the room, tracking snow as he came.

"I'm not sure yet. You have a bag for this gun?"

Clarkie felt his pockets. "There might be one here somewhere." He produced a plastic ziplock bag that maybe would hold a derringer. "How's that?" he asked.

"Dig deeper."

He dug deeper and came up with a bread sack. We stretched it to fit the target pistol.

"Thanks," I said.

"Is that all you wanted me for?"

"No. I think you should dust the house for prints. Do you have your equipment along?"

"It's in the trunk."

"Good."

"Anything else I can do while I'm here?"

"Not while you're here. But when you get home, call Sheriff Roberts in Omaha and tell him to stand by. We might need him here soon."

107

"How soon?"

"Yesterday."

"He's not going to be happy about that."

"Tell me something I don't already know."

While Clarkie dusted for fingerprints, I carried the sign and the print to Jessie and put them in the back seat. From there I drove straight to the farm and slid open the barn door. As I did, a couple pigeons swooped by in their hurry to escape. That was all I needed to announce my arrival.

The sack of food sat where I'd left it. It had gone untouched, which meant Annie had probably gone hungry rather than eat my offering.

A sparrow sailed by overhead, perched nervously on the hay hook over the mow, then sped to the other end of the barn. A second sparrow repeated the action. When an orange cat bailed out of the mow like his tail was on fire, I had to wonder who was up there.

After climbing the ladder, I started up a stack of hay bales toward the top of the mow. I never saw the bale coming until it was too late. It slammed into me, knocking me to the floor. Several other bales rained down on me. Lying there stunned, I thought I saw something black flash by on its way outside. It was one of two things—a panther or Annie Lawson.

A couple of minutes later I stood and brushed myself off. Except for my right shoulder, which I'd bruised again, I was okay. With both eyes wide open, I continued my climb to the top of the mow.

Annie wasn't there. But I found the spot, still warm, where she'd been sitting. I found something else, too, hidden between bales in a pile of loose hay. A small wooden suitcase had the initials L.R.G. carved on it. Leo R. Gohler, I bet.

Inside, I found the bare essentials—a pair of plain white panties, a stiff white bra, a pair of white athletic socks, toothbrush, toothpaste, and a bar of Ivory soap. No comb and no makeup.

At the bottom of the suitcase a small wooden box bore the same letters, L.R.G., and contained the finest set of drawing pencils I'd ever seen. Beneath the box was a pad of drawing paper and beneath the paper a set of wildlife sketches that Annie had drawn.

Edith Gohler was right. Annie had talent. Seeing into its heart and then into its soul, she had first become that which she drew; then sheathing her fangs, retracting her claws, and gripping the pencil with a remarkably human hand, she had drawn herself inside out, the way she had done with me. All she needed to become a complete artist was time—time to realize her own style, and the courage of a Leo Gohler to stay with it no matter what.

All of Annie's drawings intrigued me, for in each I saw something of her. But when I came to her sketch of a timber wolf, I had to smile. Even as he snarled, his eyes laughed, as if to say, "Here's looking at *you*, kid."

Beneath the timber wolf, at the bottom of the stack, I found the drawing Edith Gohler had told me about. It was a jackal with a man's face. Looking into his eyes, I saw the soul of evil itself, a ruthless malevolence both clever and cunning, and supremely confident of its own righteousness. It brought home to me Will Cripe's words about the leopard and his spots. Not only evil, the face was also familiar. From his slick black hair to his thin mustache to the scar that ran from his eye to his chin, it was the face of Reverend Charles Lawson, Annie's husband.

I put the sketches back where I'd found them. Thumbing through the drawing pad, I came upon a work in progress, that of a doe. Unlike the wolf, the doe's eyes didn't laugh. Hard and glazed, with terror upon them, they reminded me of Annie's eyes the first time I saw her.

12

At home Ruth sat at the kitchen table still dressed in her robe and slippers. She glanced at the pointers and fly fisherman and asked, "Where did you get those?"

"Will Cripe's. He wanted me to have them."

"He's dead?"

"No. He's missing, presumed dead."

"By whom?"

"Me."

"I'm sorry to hear that."

"That makes two of us." I laid the fisherman and pointers down on the dining room buffet. "I'll be at my office," I said.

"What about breakfast?"

"I'll wait for lunch."

"Suit yourself. But you know how you get."

I did know how I got if I missed breakfast. I decided to have a bowl of cereal and a glass of juice before I left. It was the least I could do for the citizens of Oakalla.

"Want to tell me about it?" Ruth said.

"I wish I could, Ruth. Will was supposed to meet with Annie last night, but I'm not sure whether he ever did or not. He met with someone. Or someone met with him. That much I'm sure of. Whoever it was, I think Will challenged him and got killed in the process."

"Do you think it was Annie?"

111

"No. Will loved Annie, as, I think, she loved him."

Ruth gave me a knowing look. "I see."

I shrugged. Sometimes she saw more than I wanted her to.

"Who do you think killed Will?" she asked.

"Charles Lawson, Annie's husband. I believe he's back in Oakalla."

"Is that possible?"

"I don't know, Ruth. That's what I'm asking you."

"Then maybe I'd better call Aunt Emma before the day gets too far gone, or in this case, Aunt Emma."

Ruth's Aunt Emma, though a storehouse of knowledge, was an alcoholic. At least Ruth said she was, and I'd never known Ruth to lie.

"What does Aunt Emma have to do with it?" I asked.

"She lives right across the street from the Fair Haven parsonage. Has for all of her life, even before it was a parsonage. If anybody would remember Charles Lawson, she would." She got up to make the phone call. "In the meantime, what else do you want to know about him?"

"First, I want to know if he's still alive. If he is, I want to know exactly where he can be found. If he's anywhere close, I especially need to know that."

Ruth dialed, listened momentarily, then slammed down the receiver. "Busy," she said, returning to the table.

"The story of my life."

"Keep your chin up."

"I'm trying."

Spencer Davis had my photographs ready. I paid him, thanked him, and left. Another day perhaps we could sit and reminisce.

Paul Peters stood behind the counter of the jewelry store, stifling a yawn. He saw me come in but didn't notice me right away. It was a trait he'd perfected over time.

"Good morning, Garth. What may I do for you?"

I looked at his hands, resting on the top of the jewelry case. Once they left the keyboard all the power left them. In here they appeared limp and soft.

"Will Cripe is missing," I said.

"What has that to do with me?"

"Nothing, I hope. I just wanted to let you know."

"Why?"

"Two people in Oakalla loved Annie Lawson. Will was one of them. You're the other. Now he's missing. I don't want you to end up missing, too."

"Who told you Will was in love with Annie?"

"He did."

"She wasn't in love with him."

"You might want to believe that, Paul. I might even want to believe that. But we'd both be wrong."

"How do you know it's Annie?" Though his voice was low and calm, his fingers were poised on the glass, as if ready to play.

I took her photograph out of my pocket and laid it on the jewelry case. "You be the judge."

His fingers walked across the case toward the photograph. Nimble and quick, they reminded me of a wolf spider on the prowl. But when they reached the photograph, they stopped, afraid to take the last irrevocable step.

"It's not Annie," he said hoarsely.

"Then who is it?"

"I don't know. I've never seen her before in my life."

"Will said it was Annie."

He swept the photograph off the glass, and it sailed to the far corner of the room. "He was a sick old man!" Paul exploded. "What did he know!"

"He knew Annie," I said.

Beulah Peters almost ran over me on her way into the jewelry store. "Bart!" she said. "You seem to be everywhere these days!"

Beulah wore her Cossack's hat, fur coat, and five-buckle overshoes. She looked ready to do battle with the enemy, whoever we might be.

"You have time to look at a photograph?" I asked.

"Barely. I'm scheduled to address the DAR within the hour.

113

I only stopped by here because Paul and I left some unfinished business at home."

"It'll only take a minute." I beat Paul to the photograph and handed it to her. "Recognize her?" I asked.

Beulah held the photograph out in front of her, moving it to and fro until she got it in focus. Then her rouge-red cheeks became crimson. "Of course I recognize her! That's the little tramp who had her hooks into Paul! Where did you get this? I thought I was rid of her for good!"

"Mother," Paul's voice was low and guarded, "that's not Annie."

"Of course it is! Don't you think I recognize the little slut? You should. You spent enough time mooning over her."

"Shut up," Paul said. And he meant it.

"What did you say to me?"

"I said to shut up. You don't know what you're talking about—in general, but about Annie in particular. She wasn't a slut, in fact the farthest thing from it. And if you ever open your mouth about her again, I'll put my fist into it."

"Well, I never!" Beulah threw the photograph at me and stalked out of the store.

For the second time I picked up Annie's photograph from the floor. Fortunately, it wasn't damaged.

"Your mother seems to think this is Annie Lawson," I said.

"That's her opinion."

"Why don't you?"

He didn't answer.

"If it helps any," I said, "Will loved her in the same way you did. I don't think there was anything physical between them."

"It doesn't help any. In fact, it makes it worse. I knew Annie had to sleep with her husband. That was a given. But I thought her soul belonged to me." He looked and spoke like a dead man, like he'd had his last cherished hope cruelly and irrevocably crushed. "May I see the photograph again?"

"If you promise not to destroy it."

He took the photograph from me and studied it. As he did,

114

his face softened. I felt new respect for Paul Peters. Hope died hard for some of us.

"All these years," he said, "I waited for her to come back. Otherwise, what was the point in anything." He reluctantly handed the photograph back to me. "It appears I waited for nothing."

"Have you seen her?" I asked.

"Yes. Yesterday afternoon at Fair Haven Church. I went in the morning but Sommerville Cooper was there. So I went back."

"Was it you I saw Tuesday morning in your mother's car there at the church?"

He was suddenly evasive. "Yes. The piano needed tuning."

"Then why didn't you stay and tune it?"

"It started snowing. I knew how mother would be if I got her car stuck out at Fair Haven Church."

That was a good answer, though I didn't believe it. But I didn't press him. I needed to know what he'd learned from Annie.

"You said you saw Annie. How is she?" I asked.

He shrugged. "Fine, I guess. She was in Cooper's office, trying to straighten the mess. She let me help her."

I felt uneasy, but I didn't know why. "She didn't run away from you?"

He shook his head. "No. I almost wish she had. She acted like she had nothing to fear from me, like I was a part of the church itself."

"She also might have trusted you," I said. "Like she would an old friend."

"Friend, yes . . ." His bittersweet smile betrayed him. "Well, you know what I mean."

I knew what he meant. I'd been in love alone a time or two myself.

He looked down at his hands, soft and impotent upon the jewelry glass. "I just wish I'd known that eight years ago."

"Sniffy Smith says he once saw Annie so angry she could

115

have killed her husband. He says you were there at the time." I studied Paul for his reaction, hoping he wouldn't deny it.

"Do you know why she was so angry with him?" Paul asked. "It was because he stopped me on the street, here in broad daylight in front of everyone, to accuse Annie and me of having an affair behind his back. For Annie's sake I tried to laugh it off. But she was furious with him. I'd never seen her so angry. Partly it was in my defense, but more, I think, it was because he accused her of being unfaithful. Annie, who didn't know the meaning of the word."

"What did she do?"

"Nothing. She was so angry she couldn't talk, which was hard for her anyway. She tried to beat on him with her fists, but he kept her at bay. Finally she just turned and walked back the way they'd come, jerking her arm away whenever he tried to stop her."

"What did you do?"

"Watched them go, of course." His smile was brutally self-mocking. "Paul Peters never gets involved."

"How long after that did Lawson and Annie leave town?" I asked.

"That same night."

"I see."

"Then you also see Annie's danger, now that she has come back."

"Danger from whom?"

But he wouldn't answer. Paul Peters had told me all he was going to.

13

At my office I called Edith Gohler in Four Corners. She might have been in the tower. It took several rings before she answered the phone.

"This is Garth Ryland in Oakalla. I was there the other day."

"Yes, I remember you. You own one of Leo's paintings."

"You also remember I came about Mary?"

"Yes. Is it she you found?"

"Yes. Her real name is Annie Lawson. Does that mean anything to you?"

"No. Should it?"

"Probably not. But I wanted to make sure."

"Is Mary well?"

"As well as can be expected. But some unusual events have taken place recently. I'm sure she's somehow involved."

"What kind of unusual events?" she asked, concerned.

"One disappearance. One violent attack that I know of."

"And you think it's Mary?"

"No," I said with certainty.

"Thank you."

I allowed myself a smile. Edith Gohler loved Annie more than she knew. But then, didn't we all.

"I do need your help, though," I said. "Do you remember if she ever left the house at night?"

"Night was the only time she would leave. Sometimes she wouldn't get back until morning."

"From the beginning, or did her outings gradually lengthen?"

"No. Not at first. At first she would hardly leave her room. But over time she began to explore more of the house. Then one night, much to my surprise, she went outside. I held my breath, wondering what would happen. She returned a few minutes later, apparently none the worse for it. From then on I couldn't keep her in the house at night, and as more time passed, her strays became longer and longer."

"Where did she go?"

"I never followed her. But one of my neighbors thought he saw her clear over on State Road 13 one night. When he stopped to make sure, she disappeared."

"That's nearer Oakalla than Four Corners."

"What are you saying, Mr. Ryland?"

"I'm no expert on amnesia. But I think Mary's been working her way back to Oakalla a step at a time. I don't know for certain why. She might not even know."

"Have you talked to Mary?"

"I've tried. She won't let me get close enough to do any good."

"I'm sorry. I can't help you. Leo could, if he were here. He always saw things so clearly." She spoke about Leo the way Ruth often spoke about Karl, her late husband—as if he were still a part of her.

"Too clearly?"

"It's better not to see too much, Mr. Ryland. Especially if one is an artist."

"And paints only barns?"

"His critics never forgave him. It was a waste, they said, of his talent."

"What did Leo say?"

"Leo said it wasn't barns he painted. It was life. The barn was only there to frame it."

"Well said."

"Leo's words. Not mine."

I hung up and began pulling back issues of *Freedom's Voice*, the forerunner of the *Oakalla Reporter*. If Annie Lawson was in Oakalla eight years ago, there ought to be a photograph of her and her husband.

The closest thing I could find to it was the announcement in the June 16, 1978, edition that Reverend Charles Lawson was to fill the pulpit at Fair Haven Church. A native of Kentucky, it said, he was the son of a minister and had been preaching himself these past twenty years. But there was no mention of his wife and no photograph.

From June 16, 1978, I went forward week by week, until I came to the brief announcement in the July 20, 1979, edition that services at Fair Haven Church were cancelled until further notice. No explanation was given.

All in all it seemed strange that neither Annie's picture nor that of her husband ever made it into *Freedom's Voice*. It would have seemed stranger had Beulah Peters not been its owner.

The phone rang. It was Clarkie, and he sounded upset. "Garth, you'd better get out here right away!"

"Where are you?"

"Will Cripe's house. I got a match on the prints and came back to dust for more. But somebody's made a holy mess out of the place."

"I'll be there as soon as I can."

On my way home to get Jessie, I glanced in the window of the jewelry store. Paul Peters wasn't inside.

I opened the door and asked Bill Nicewander, the owner, where Paul had gone.

"Home, I reckon," he said. "I'd stepped out for coffee at the Corner, and when I got back, he was gone. No note or anything. He left the place wide open for whoever might wander in."

"Is that unusual?"

"Unusual in that he's never done it before when I wasn't here. You know Paul. Sometimes his mind gets the best of him, and he has to step outside, smoke a cigarette, and let himself calm down a little. But he's never just up and left before without telling me he was going."

"How long ago did he leave?"

"I have no idea."

"Thanks, Bill."

Clarkie was right. Somebody had savaged Will Cripe's house with a vengeance that more than matched his ransacking of Coop's office. Drawers had been opened and their contents dumped, furniture overturned, and a few of Will's keepsakes—including his prize decoy, a bluewing teal—had been broken. There was no way to tell what all was missing. One thing I knew for certain: Will's .30-.30 Winchester that hung above the fireplace. But I didn't know when it had been taken, because I didn't remember seeing it for sure earlier that morning.

"What do you think?" Clarkie said.

"I don't know what to think. You say you have a match?"

"Yes. With one of the two sets of prints I found on the pistol."

"You run them through your computer yet?"

"The ball's rolling, but I haven't come up with anything. It's a long shot you realize. There's no way to identify either set of prints, unless he has a record."

"Well, do your best."

"That's not all. Someone tried to fire that pistol recently. There are marks on two of the shells where the firing pin hit. You can tell it's recent because the brass is still shiny."

"Why didn't the shells fire?"

"Wet powder. I took one apart to look at it. I had to use an ice pick to even get the powder out."

"Save the other," I said. "It might be evidence."

"Of what?"

"Will's murder. You called Sheriff Roberts yet?"

"I called the number he gave me. No one answered."

"Try again. If you don't have any luck, call the Omaha police and have them track him down. In the meantime stop by Paul Peters' house and see if he's there. If he's not, find out where he went when he left the jewelry store this morning. I'll be at my office in case you come up with anything."

"You leaving now?"

"In a minute. I want to make a phone call first."

I followed Clarkie to the kitchen where I called Coop at his home.

Coop must have been standing by the phone. He answered right away.

"Coop, this is Garth. I just wanted to apologize for what happened earlier today. I don't know what got into me, but I'm sorry."

"You don't have to apologize. I wasn't myself either. Someone slipped a note under my door during the night. I found it when I returned from Ricelander."

"Same message as before?"

"About the same. More virulent, if anything."

"And you still have no idea who wrote it?"

"I now have an idea, Garth. But I don't think I should share it with you. The man in question is not to be taken lightly."

"Charles Lawson?"

Dead silence from his end.

"Coop, you there?"

"I am always amazed," he said, "what the mention of that name does to me. But as a friend, I'll ask you to leave this quest up to me. Annie's life depends on it."

"I did that and lost a friend in the bargain. Not again."

He sighed. "Do as you must. I'll do the same."

"Would you answer this question for me?" I said. "Why did you go to Ricelander last night?"

"You remember I served there before I came here. My congregation has never really accepted my leaving or their new minister. I went there on a goodwill mission."

"To preach at a revival?"

"Yes. Unlike yours, there are still some lost souls out there."

"And you have no idea why Will wanted to talk to you last night?"

"Yes. Now that I've had a chance to think about it. He

121

mentioned to me once about leaving his property to Fair Haven Church. Perhaps he wanted to confirm that offer to me."

I glanced at the bluewing teal, its head severed from its body. "That means he knew he was about to die."

"I'm sorry, Garth. That thought also came to mind."

Before I left, I took one last look around the house. No matter how hard he'd tried—and the destruction was nearly complete—whoever had done this couldn't erase the memories, couldn't make Will Cripe less of a man. The fact that he had even tried made me believe it could only be Charles Lawson.

Beulah Peters' white Cadillac was still at Fair Haven Church. Beulah stood in the sanctuary, replacing all the white candles with red ones. She hummed as she worked. "Onward Christian Soldiers."

"Hello, Beulah. The DAR like your speech?"

She spun around to face me, then put her hand over her heart. "Bart! You just took ten years off my life."

"I thought you heard me come in. I guess you didn't."

"I told Paul to lock the door on his way out. You can see how well he listens to me." She replaced a white candle with a red one.

"Paul was here?"

"Yes. And somebody else, too. He left the basement door wide open."

"What was Paul doing here?"

She looked at me with complete understanding. "The same thing you're doing here, Garth. Looking for Annie."

That was the first time she'd ever called me Garth. Her look said it wasn't a slip of the tongue. "Did he find her?" I asked.

"No." She sat down on the altar where I joined her. "Two weeks ago today, that was the start of it." Her voice fell. "When he played *her* song, instead of mine."

"Her song?"

"You know which one it is. 'I come to the garden alone, while the dew is still on the roses . . .' It's the one I sang at your grandmother's funeral. Against my better judgment, I might add."

"Why against your better judgment?" I asked.

"Think about it, Garth. How many Leonardos have there been? And who would be fool enough to try to outdo him at what he did best?"

"Like the Mona Lisa?"

"That'll do for a starter."

"Then why did you do it?" I asked.

"Two reasons. Anna Marie Ryland was an old friend. And no one else had the guts to."

"But Paul wouldn't accompany you on the piano."

"No. He thought no one but Annie should ever sing that song." She spoke quietly, more to herself than to me. "It was the first song, you see, that they ever did together. I knew right then I was in for the fight of my life."

"For Paul?"

"Of course, for Paul!" she snapped, coming back to life. "Who do you think I've been talking about?" She rose and dusted herself off, replacing another candle.

"I was thinking about something else," I admitted. "If Paul didn't think anyone but Annie should sing her song, then why did he suddenly start playing it two weeks ago?"

"That's the sixty-four-thousand–dollar question. At first I thought it was just to spite me. God knows he played that song enough after she left. For a year that's about all I heard. But the look on his face said no, it wasn't out of spite. Paul wasn't even conscious of what he was doing. The song just came to him out of the blue."

"Or out of the past," I suggested.

"What do you mean, out of the past?" She opened another box of red candles and continued replacing the white ones.

"I'm not sure what I mean, Beulah. But Paul is an artist, and artists don't see things the way the rest of us do. They're more in tune to the subtleties of life. Paul might have been taking his cue from something that no one else recognized."

"Like what?"

"I don't know. Did anything happen that night at choir practice that might have set him off?"

She thought about it, then said, "Just the usual. Sommerville Cooper gave us the songs he planned to use in the service. We practiced those a time or two; then when it was time for me to sing my song, Paul went off on his tangent."

"What exactly is your song?" I asked.

"It's not mine really," she admitted. "I just sing it because I know Paul likes to play it. It's the one with all the fanfare throughout it. You know, the one that begs for trumpets . . ." She hummed a phrase.

"'God of Our Fathers.'"

"That's it! Paul had just finished the introduction and I was all set to sing, when what comes out? *Her* song. Now you tell me, unless she was already on his mind, how Paul got from here to there."

"I can't," I said. "But maybe Paul can."

"Good luck. That's all I can say. I've been after him for the past two weeks to tell me what's going on. He claims he doesn't know."

"Maybe he doesn't know exactly. Like me, he might be fumbling around in the dark. You say someone else was here before you and left the basement door open?"

"Yes. I thought I heard someone in there." She nodded toward Coop's office. "Then the chancel door closed. It was later, when I went looking for candles, that I found the basement door open."

"Excuse me a minute, Beulah."

Coop's office had been ransacked again, even worse than before. Books and papers were strewn all over the floor, while some of the books had their covers ripped off and pages torn out. I felt doubly angry, for Annie's sake because all of her caring work had been undone, and for Coop who had to pick up the pieces once more.

Beulah came up behind me and gasped when she saw the destruction. We exchanged looks, each asking the same question: why?

"Did Paul see this mess?" I asked.

Beulah knelt to retrieve a Bible, then tried to piece it back

124

together. "Yes. He must have. The office was the first place he stopped. But he told me nothing about *this.*"

With good reason, I thought.

I offered my hand and pulled her to her feet. "Do me a favor, Beulah. Change your candles another day. It's not safe here."

For the first time since I'd known her, Beulah Peters agreed with me. "Perhaps you're right, Garth."

I walked with her as far as the front door. "You said when you first saw Paul and Annie perform together, you knew you were in for the fight of your life. What exactly did you mean, Beulah?"

"Paul's career. He was all set to go to the Juilliard school of music when he met Annie. After that he lost all interest in going."

"Even after she left Oakalla?"

"Especially after she left Oakalla. He kept awaiting her return."

"Now I understand," I said, meaning Paul.

She looked worn and confused, and most of all, vulnerable. "I wish I did."

I drove back to Oakalla, ate a late lunch at the Corner Bar and Grill, and went to my office to work on the *Oakalla Reporter*. Afternoon passed into evening, evening into night.

Along Gas Line Road I could see the declarations of Christmas: outside lights and inside lights, candles and candy canes, shepherds, Rudolphs, wise men, and Santas. And somewhere in my office yard, though it was now too dark to see, the stump of Frosty the Snowman.

Still in my typewriter was this week's column. So far I'd been unable to finish it.

I remembered my first sled, a Silver Streak, my first bicycle, my first and only Daisy BB gun. I remembered starring in my first Christmas operetta and my last Christmas operetta, how magical the world had seemed at age seven, how much it had changed by age twelve. I remembered my first Christmas at Grandmother Ryland's and my first Christmas without her. I remembered my first Christmas present to Diana and the unspoken love in her eyes, and I remembered her first Christmas present to me, the oak-framed copy of my very first *Oakalla Reporter* that had hung above my desk ever since. I remembered what I wanted to feel, but was unable to feel it, as though someone else had lived my life, then willed me its memories.

Picking up Annie Lawson's photograph, I held it up to the light. Surprise showed on her face. I'd caught her at an unguarded moment when she thought no one was looking. It should have been revealing. It wasn't. Neither were the other two photographs I'd snapped of her.

In contrast, the drawing she'd made of me looked into my soul, showed me what I'd only hoped was there. That was the difference between art and life.

14

Reaching across my desk to answer the phone, I realized my right arm wasn't working yet. I had clubs for fingers and a rock imbedded in my shoulder. The second thing I realized was that it was still dark outside, somewhere between midnight and dawn. I knew trouble was calling.

"Garth, this is Beulah Peters. I'm worried. It's five o'clock and Paul hasn't come home yet."

"Home from where?" I switched the phone from my right hand to my left and began a slow windmill to try to loosen my right shoulder. I could hear it grind inside.

"I don't know. I haven't seen him since yesterday afternoon at the church."

"He wasn't at choir practice?" I knew it was scheduled for Thursday night.

"We didn't have choir practice. Sommerville Cooper took one look at his office, then called me to cancel it and told me to call the others."

"I'll look into it, Beulah."

"Thanks, Garth." Her voice was close to breaking. "I didn't know where else to turn."

After wrestling with my coat, I went outside and climbed into Jessie. True to form, she wouldn't turn over. It was her way of saying thanks for leaving her out all night in the cold.

I looked around the neighborhood and saw no one up and

about; thought about calling Ruth but decided against it. The only thing left to do was to walk uptown to the Marathon and wait for Danny, who always opened up early.

Fortunately, he arrived at the same time I did. He gave me a ride back to my office where we jumped Jessie, then brought her to the station for a quick charge.

While waiting, I drank a cup of coffee from Danny's thermos and ate one of his jelly-filled rolls. If worse came to worse, that would be my breakfast.

At dawn I arrived at Fair Haven Church. Paul Peters' black 280 ZX was parked in the lot, but Paul wasn't in it. Inside the church I made the circuit from sanctuary to choir room to basement to vestibule without finding him. I finally ended up in Coop's office. No one had righted it since I was last in there.

I called Clarkie and got him out of bed. "Clarkie, this is Garth. You reached Sheriff Roberts yet?"

"Not yet. I called the Omaha police like you said. Nobody is there at his brother-in-law's."

"Keep trying. It's time he came home."

"What now?"

"Paul Peters has disappeared. His mother called me early this morning."

"Disappeared from where?"

"I don't know. I'm out at Fair Haven Church now. Paul's car is here, but he's nowhere to be found. It doesn't look good, Clarkie."

"I'll put in a call to Sheriff Roberts now."

"Good. I'll wait here until I hear from you."

Five minutes later Clarkie called me back. "Sorry, Garth, they still don't answer the phone."

"Damn!"

"That's just the half of it," he went on. "Have you looked at a weather map lately? There's a hell of a snowstorm coming up from the southwest. It's due to hit Omaha tonight. . . ." He let that sink in, then asked, "So do you want me to stay here and keep trying to reach him?"

128

"No. I want you to make the rounds and find out if anyone has seen Paul Peters since late yesterday afternoon."

"Where will you be in case I need to get hold of you?"

"At my office."

"All day?"

"However long it takes."

"To do what?"

"I ran Annie Lawson's photograph in the *Reporter*. I want to see what comes of it."

"What are you hoping for?"

"I don't know, Clarkie. Maybe I will by the end of the day."

"I tried to find Paul Peters yesterday afternoon like you said. . . ." His voice trailed. "If only I'd stuck with it."

"Don't worry about it, Clarkie. When it comes to might-have-beens, I'm right in there with you."

"At least we're in good company."

I had to smile. "The best."

After we hung up, I called Ruth at home. The last time I'd talked to her was the previous evening to tell her I wouldn't be home for supper and probably not the rest of the night. She wasn't surprised. We'd been over this road before.

"Where are you?" she asked.

"Fair Haven Church. Paul Peters has disappeared. His car's here, but he's not."

"That's not good news."

"No. Not good news at all. Anything happening on your end?"

"Not much. Charles Lawson, Annie's husband, has fallen off the edge of the earth. I can't find hide nor hair of him anywhere for the past eight years."

"You've checked all your sources?"

"All that I can reach. From here he went nowhere that I can find. I even checked with all the churches around the area. The preachers that do remember him would just as soon forget him. But they haven't seen him either."

"Have you checked out of state, Kentucky in particular?"

"I've checked there and all points south."

"Any further word on Annie's parents?"

"No. I've been too busy trying to track Charles Lawson down. Do you want me to shift gears?"

"No. I want you to exhaust every possibility before you give up."

"I'm about to that stage now. There is one possibility you don't want to consider, that Charles Lawson never left town."

"I've considered it, Ruth. I just don't believe it."

"Why? What has Annie given you, besides grief?"

I thought about Annie's voice, its purity and its unabashed joy for life. "Reason for hope. That's all I can say."

"Not a small thing."

"No. Not a small thing at all."

Hope was all I had until Sam Licklightner walked into my office shortly before noon. Sam was a retired electrician who had since kept busy dodging his old customers, playing golf, and scouring all the old haunts around Oakalla with his metal detector. On at least two occasions he and I had gone treasure hunting together at places where I was sure we would find something worthwhile. But, except for fellowship and some good-natured ribbing, we had come up empty. Rupert suggested, and I concurred, that it was because Sam had been over that same ground before.

"Morning, Garth," he said.

"Morning, Sam. What brings you here?"

He handed me that day's edition of the *Oakalla Reporter*, the one with Annie's photograph in it, and the question: "Do you know this woman?"

"This brings me here," Sam said. Then he laid a gold locket on top of the paper. "And this."

I opened the locket. There were two facing photographs inside, those of a man and a woman. The man had slick black hair, a thin black mustache waxed at the ends, a scar on his left cheek, and dark, deep-set eyes. He looked to be in his forties. He also looked like he'd never smiled in his life.

130

The woman opposite him was little more than a girl. She had wispy blond hair, large blue eyes, and a face as lovely as it was vulnerable.

Transfixed, I sat staring at her, unable to lay the locket down. She touched a younger, self-important me, and made him want to pick up his sword and defend her to the death. I was glad I hadn't known her back then. She was just the kind of woman I didn't need. She was Annie Lawson.

"When and where did you find this?" I asked.

"A couple years ago up around that old house on Hoover's Ridge." He handed me a thin gold necklace. "I found this with it."

I examined the necklace. It was broken. "Two years ago you say?"

"That's close enough. I was up there with my metal detector looking for old coins. I found these instead."

"It looks like the necklace goes with the locket."

"That'd be my guess."

"Do you mind if I hang onto them for a while?" I asked.

"For five bucks you can hang on to them forever."

"They're worth a lot more than that."

"Maybe so. But that's all I'm asking."

"Why?" I asked, mainly because Sam Licklightner had the reputation of never giving anybody anything.

"I've got my own reasons." Ones I wasn't going to hear.

I took a twenty-dollar bill from my wallet and handed it to him. "Thank you, Sam."

"I only asked for five," he reminded me.

"That's all the change I have."

"I should be so lucky." He stopped at the door on his way out. "Who is she?" he asked.

"The girl in the locket?"

"Yes."

"Her name is Annie Lawson. She lived here about eight years ago."

"She sure is a beauty, isn't she?"

"Yes, Sam, she sure is."

Sam had no sooner left than Coop came into the office carrying a copy of the *Oakalla Reporter*. He stood facing me across my desk. He didn't look happy to be here.

"Yes, Coop, what is it?"

"The girl in the paper is Annie Pate, the one I married."

"I know."

"Why did you run her picture for all of Oakalla to see?"

"Here's one of the reasons." I handed him the locket Sam Licklightner had given me. It had the same effect on Coop as it'd had on me. He stood transfixed, unable to lift his eyes from Annie's face.

"Are those the two people you married?" I asked.

He didn't answer. He slowly shook his large head back and forth, like an old lion who had lost his pride. As that day at the church when she sang to us, there were tears in his eyes.

"Coop?"

He raised his head, staring through me at the wall beyond. "I'm sorry, Garth. What was the question again?"

"Are those the two people you married?"

"Yes. With regret." For once all of his bluster was gone. Like that day at the church, I felt like I was seeing the real Coop for a brief time. But Annie had that power. By her presence alone, she brought out the best and the worst in us. Was it a desire to possess her? Or was it something in her that we responded to, something that went beyond beauty as we defined it? The sum of her—the life force that even in repose could not be denied.

"Why do you say with regret?" I asked.

"Look at her, Garth. She's just a child. Now look at the man she married."

"Not a pretty face," I said. "But not necessarily the face of evil."

He shook his head. "I can't even begin to explain."

"Try. It's important I understand."

"It's beyond you, Garth. Believe me."

"I believe you. I still want you to try to explain." I got up

132

and brought him a chair. "And sit down while you're doing it. It'll seem less like preaching."

"You mean I'll be less likely to preach."

"That too."

He sat down in the chair, but he wasn't comfortable there. He missed the weight of the pulpit.

"I was a friend of Annie's family," he began. "I had been for years. From bud to rose I'd watched her blossom, hating the man I knew would someday pick her. But I hoped, prayed to God he would be a kind and gentle man, one who would treat her with the love and adoration she deserved, one who would realize what a true prize he had."

He stopped. I was afraid he wouldn't go on.

"Then along came Charles Lawson," I said.

"Yes. Along came Charles Lawson. Strange that I can speak his name now, while all these years I couldn't. It is as though when Annie married him I struck his name from my mind, never to be spoken again."

"Why *did* Annie marry him? Do you have an answer for that?"

"Look at him!" Coop held out the locket for me to see. "Can't you see the power there? The power of darkness. You should have heard him speak, Garth. He could make the faintest of heart rise up and shout, Hallelujah! Hallelujah!" As he spoke, Coop rose from his chair and his face hardened. He had that moment become Charles Lawson. And he was right. There was power in darkness.

"And when he moved," Coop began to prowl around the room, "he moved like a cat. Sleek and sure without a wasted motion. Oh, he was something. Annie had no chance against him." He stood staring out the window into the past. He seemed to have forgotten I was there.

"Coop? Are you with me?"

He turned to look at me. As he did, his face reddened. "Sorry, Garth. You asked me not to preach." He returned to sit in the chair across from me.

"So Annie was truly an innocent?"

133

"Yes. She was the meaning of the word."

"Then why didn't you use your influence with her to try to stop her marriage?"

"I did. As much as I was able. But Annie's will is her own. She wouldn't listen to me."

"There's also the possibility Annie knew exactly what she was getting in Charles Lawson. That she chose him for that very reason," I said.

"No! As God is my witness, he deceived her!"

"Coop, you said yourself she was the danger."

"To me! Not to anyone else. She was a danger to my spirit. I know I betrayed her."

"You said she has her own mind. How could you betray her?"

He shook his head. "I did, that's all."

"Then tell me about Charles Lawson," I said.

"I told you about him. He was Satan's apostle."

"That doesn't tell me much. I understand his father was a minister."

"Who told you that?"

"I read it in *Freedom's Voice*. It was the forerunner of the *Oakalla Reporter*."

"He was *here*? In Oakalla?"

"Didn't you already know that? Isn't that why you're here?"

"What exactly do you mean, Garth?"

"I mean you came here looking for Annie. It's too much of a coincidence to explain otherwise. What did she do, write you from here? That's how you knew to come to Oakalla?"

He looked hard at me, but I wouldn't look away. Finally I stared him down.

"What about Charles Lawson?" I asked. "Have you heard anything about him?"

"No. Not until recently."

"You mean the letters you received?"

"Yes."

"Was his father a minister, like the article says he was?"

"Yes. I knew his father well. He was a kindly though distant

134

man, perhaps better suited for pharmacy than the rigors of the ministry. He died young, when Charles was in his teens."

"What about Charles's mother?"

"He hardly knew his mother. She ran off with a salesman when he was a boy. He fell under the care of his maiden aunt, who did not spare the rod but spoiled the child."

"Charles told you this?"

"He once confided in me, yes. When he was younger, fresh in the calling. As he grew older, he grew more distant and sullen, more enamored with his own power."

"Did your paths often cross?"

"Often, while we were in Kentucky. It seemed I was always in his wake, trying to undo the harm he had done. Though he called a great many to the service of the Lord, he lacked the wherewithal to sustain their faith. By the time I arrived I found it badly shaken, the church and its members at war with one another."

"Like Fair Haven?"

"Like Fair Haven. Even if I had no idea he had ever been here eight years ago, after seeing the church and its people, I would have known. The seeds he sows bear bitter fruit."

"Anything else about him I should know?" I asked.

"He's a vengeful man. Though he preaches forgiveness, he himself does not practice it. If he *is* here in Oakalla, give him wide berth. He will not forget an injury."

"You have any proof of that?"

"Rumor is all, though I believe it. That he once killed a man in a knife fight."

"Who was the man?"

"His first wife's lover."

"What happened to her?"

"She disappeared. No one has seen her since."

I felt the temperature in the room drop about ten degrees. "Thanks, Coop, for stopping by."

He rose and started for the door.

"Coop?"

He stopped. "Yes, Garth?"

135

"Could I have the locket back? I'm not through with it yet."

"Of course."

He left with his head bowed and his shoulders bent.

An hour passed. I was about to go to lunch when Ruth's Aunt Emma hobbled in on her cane, carrying her Bible. As she flopped into the chair Coop had vacated, it seemed every one of her bones cracked. She didn't bother to take off her coat. It was enough of a chore to pull off her orange stocking cap.

"So," she said, pointing her cane at me. "You're back to stirring up things again."

"It looks like it," I said.

"About time somebody did. This town's getting duller by the minute." She gave the chair a scornful look. "You don't count on people staying long, do you?"

"How's that?"

"This chair. It's harder than Ruth's candy."

I smiled in sympathy.

"I know her," Aunt Emma said. "The girl in the paper."

"I was hoping you would."

"She lived across the street from me. About a year all told. Then I heard a ruckus one night, saw a car drive off, and never saw her again."

I handed her the locket. "Is this she?"

"She and her husband. Old smiley himself."

"I take it you didn't like him?"

"Why do you say that?"

"Nobody else did."

"You take it right. I never saw a man with a more sour disposition. It got so the sun wouldn't even come up if it saw him first."

"What about his sermons? How were they?"

"I don't know. I never went to hear him. Hell, fire, and brimstone would be my guess."

"Mine too. What about Annie? What was she like?"

"She stuttered for one thing. That frustrated her, so whenever she could she'd try to get around talking. She had more expressions than some people have excuses, and with every

136

one of them I knew exactly what she was thinking. Soft as a summer-puff, that was my first thought about her. But there was a lot more underneath that didn't meet the eye."

"Such as?"

"That girl was flat out bright, Garth. Even without talking, she could get from here to there faster than any human I ever met. In a hundred yard dash she'd even leave *you* at the post. But you'd probably catch up to her over the course of a mile."

"She ever confide in you?"

"About what?"

"Anything."

"She was homesick. I could tell that from the start. Heartsick, too, unless I miss my guess."

"Why was that?"

"Old smiley. Though she didn't come right out and say it, he wasn't quite the bargain she thought he was."

"Did he ever mistreat her?"

"She never said if he did. But I wouldn't put it past him." She scowled, stood, then sat back down again on top of her Bible. "What exactly are you looking for, Garth?"

"The reason why he tried to kill her."

"Who said he did?"

"It's just a theory. You say you heard a fight, then saw a car leaving a short time later. Did you see who was driving it?"

"No. I just saw its lights."

She rose from the chair and pulled her orange stocking cap down over her head until only her eyes, nose, and chin showed. "Well, if that's all, I need to get uptown. I hear we've got a doozy of a storm coming, and I'm out of cigarettes."

"Hard to eat those."

"Chew them either, though I've been down to that when I ran out of matches."

"If I remember right, you promised Ruth you'd stop smoking."

"I did for two weeks. Longest two weeks of my life. Didn't take a drink either. Went cold turkey on both. Took up walking instead. Wore blisters on both feet and a hole in the sidewalk.

That's when I said to hell with it. I'm eighty-six years old. Who am I saving myself for?"

"You never know."

"True. But you can get close enough to guess." She waved her cane at me. "Have a good one."

"One last question?"

"Shoot."

"Did you ever hear Annie sing?"

"Not at church. Sometimes when she was home alone I would."

"What did you think of her voice?"

"Like a nightingale's. I've never heard a sweeter sound."

I nodded. She waved again and left.

I walked to my window to watch her go. The sky was grey, the wind slowly pushing an oak leaf from east to west across the snow, a cluster of sparrows gathering in my cedar. Aunt Emma and Clarkie were right. A snow was coming.

Clarkie came into my office, looking perplexed as usual. "I didn't have any luck finding Paul Peters," he said. "The people I talked to don't know a thing more than we do."

"What about the fingerprints on the pistol? Any word yet?"

"No. I'm still waiting to hear."

"Keep after it, Clarkie."

"I plan to. I know it's important to you."

"You're right. It is."

"You mind me asking why."

"Will Cripe is why. I want him to go out with a bang, not a whimper."

"I'm not sure I understand."

"It's a way of looking at life, Clarkie. And death. I hate to see either wasted. Especially Will's."

He brightened. "I got you now." He started for the door.

"Do me one more favor?" I asked.

"Sure."

"Aunt Emma's on her way uptown. See that she makes it there and back okay. And while you're at it, bring me a corned beef sandwich and a carton of milk from the Corner. I'd like to stay here in case somebody else drops by."

"Anything on the corned beef?"

"Mayonnaise and sauerkraut on rye."

After he left, I waited throughout the afternoon for further word on Annie Lawson. None came.

15

I drove out to the farm at dusk. The sky was a pale grey, the wind sharp out of the northeast, but the promised storm had yet to come.

I didn't go into the barn. If Annie was there that's where I wanted her to stay. Taking a shovel and flashlight from Jessie, I walked across country to the house on Hoover's Ridge. When I got there, I stood for several minutes at the door listening. Animal sounds were all I heard. I decided to go inside.

It seemed cold in there, colder even than outside. I shined the flashlight around the room from the hearth to the new stack of wood to the blanket on the black chair. Except for the wood, nothing appeared to have changed since I was last here. But there was a different smell to the house, one that caught in my craw and stuck, one I couldn't quite place until I shined the flashlight under the house and saw where someone had been digging.

I hated that musty smell of dry rot. As a boy I'd crawled under my aunt's house to help my father jack it up and brace its floor joists. Since I was the smallest, I had to go into the tightest places, which meant digging part of the way while lying flat on my stomach, wedged between the floor and the ground. I had never done harder or dirtier work in my life.

But that wasn't the worst part. When I finally reached the foundation, I had to set the jack and jack the house up, all the while listening to the timbers creak and crack, certain one would snap and the house would come down on top of me.

I hadn't crawled very far under a house since. I wasn't sure I could do it now.

Telling myself that was years ago, I eased through a hole in the floor until I hit bottom. Sitting down, I shined the flashlight ahead of me. There was some room to maneuver under here, maybe two or three feet of space, enough to crawl but not walk. A rat hole appeared every few feet, until I shined the light on the area where someone had been digging. There the rat holes disappeared under the newly-turned earth.

Whoever it was had been thorough in his task. Starting in one corner, he'd dug his way back and forth under the house until he'd either run out of space or run out of time, or found what he was looking for. I decided to start where he'd left off.

It wasn't hard digging. The loam was light and dry, like shoveling talc. But hunched beneath the floor with a timber to my back, I never quite got my rhythm. Gradually my grip on the shovel tightened, and my muscles bound, refusing to flow.

The back door banged, followed by the creak of floorboards. Someone headed my way. Smothering the flashlight, I turned it off, then crawled to the far corner of the house. On my way my hand brushed something hard and smooth. It felt like the toe of someone's shoe.

The footfalls stopped at the hole in the floor where I'd come under the house. Click, and a flashlight came on. I turned away and tried to bury myself in the corner. Too late I realized I should have brought the shovel with me.

"Annie? Annie?" The voice took me by surprise. It was soft and high-pitched and raised the hair on my neck. "Annie? Are you there?"

Silence followed, one so deep I could hear the patter of snow on the leaves outside. Listening for Annie. The house itself seemed to be listening for Annie's answer.

"Annie?"

I jumped at the sound.

"Annie, I've brought you someone. Someone to keep you

142

warm through the cold nights ahead. Your lover, Annie. I've brought you your lover." The floorboards creaked with effort as something heavy tumbled through the hole and hit the ground. "Sweet dreams, Annie. Sweet dreams."

Footfalls moved away until I didn't hear them anymore. But I didn't move, not until my legs screamed for mercy. Then I sat down and stretched out as quietly as I could.

Paul Peter's frozen body lay beneath the hole in the floor. He looked puzzled, slightly amused, as if he hadn't seen death coming, or if he had, chose to look the other way. My guess was that he hadn't. The welt at the base of his skull seemed to confirm it.

Will Cripe was buried less than a foot down. My hand had brushed the toe of his boot while I was hiding from his killer. I didn't uncover him all the way, just far enough to look at his face.

There was no way to read it for sure, but he looked satisfied. And I now knew he hadn't died for nothing. He had flushed a killer from hiding in order to save Annie, and in so doing drawn the killer's wrath upon himself. Perhaps Will knew all along that the pistol he held under his afghan wouldn't fire but that didn't stop him. And when the shells died in the chamber, so did Will. Not his act of courage, however. It lived on to remind me that there were still those who gave their "last full measure of devotion."

I continued digging. More than ever I had to finish what I'd started. For the first time since Annie's arrival I thought I knew what was going on. But I wouldn't know for sure until I overturned every square foot of earth.

Hours passed. As I worked my way through the remaining earth, each shovelful had grown heavier until my hands were knotted into claws that would barely bend to grip the handle. Cold sweat popped out on my forehead, and my muscles gathered, wanting to run. They said to get the hell out of here while I still could. But will prevailed, and I finished my task.

Nothing. That's what I found, what I was hoping to find.

Outside, I was surprised to see the moon showing through

143

the clouds. But it was fuzzy and dim, and by the time I reached the road it had gone under again.

Looking behind me, back toward Hoover's Ridge, I could see the woods in silhouette. From the safety of the road, it was hard to believe I'd just been in there, glimpsed the face of madness, and held the hand of an old friend.

Turning on the light in the barn, I heard the flutter of birds, as first the pigeons then the sparrows rose from their perches and settled back down again. I wanted Annie to know who it was, but I didn't want to alarm her, so I stayed where I was.

"Annie, it's Garth Ryland. You're in danger here. Go back to Four Corners and wait until you hear from me. And whatever you do, stay away from Fair Haven Church."

I waited for her answer, but didn't get one.

"Annie, did you hear me? Let me know if you did."

Still no answer. She had no reason to trust me after what I'd done, but I was hoping she would.

"That's all, Annie. I'm leaving now."

After a shower I walked to Doc Airhart's. Doc lived in a large stone house across the street from the United Methodist Church. Small and trim, with snow-white hair and merry blue eyes, he was as close to a patriarch as we had in Oakalla. He was also my friend.

Doc's porch was aglow with Christmas lights from one end to the other, and his tree, a long-needled fir, looked fat and content, just like his setter, Belle, who lay on the hardwood floor beside it. Doc had a fire going and a scotch in his hand when he let me inside. The rush of smells almost overwhelmed me. For a moment, it was Christmas at Grandmother Ryland's, and I was a boy again.

"I could have used you yesterday," I said.

"How's that?"

"When I wrote my article on Christmas memories. Even under a deadline, it came out flat."

"Some days are like that. Right, Belle?"

Belle rolled over and groaned, wanting her belly scratched.

I walked over to oblige her. She closed her eyes and sighed happily.

"Don't spoil her too much," Doc said. "Otherwise, she'll come to expect it."

I smiled. I knew it was way too late for that.

"Why don't you take off your coat and stay awhile?" he said. "I've got a bottle of J & B that needs some attention."

I thought about it. Where else did I need to go tonight? Nowhere, I decided. "You care if I use your phone?"

"Help yourself. You know where it is."

I called Clarkie, but he wasn't home. He must be out patrolling.

Returning to the living room, I held my hands to the fire. I was having a hard time getting warm. The words of Lieutenant Cavanaugh kept running through my mind. "Dirty, disoriented, shell shock, foxhole . . ." So I asked Doc if Annie could have been buried alive.

"It's possible," he said. "But that's out of my league. You should ask a psychiatrist."

"I would if I knew one."

He handed me my glass of scotch. Doc knew only one way to drink it, straight up. And that's the only way he let me drink it.

"The symptoms are all there," he went on. "Shock, amnesia, autism. That's probably what I'd go through if somebody hit me on the head and buried me alive."

"So you don't think she's faking?"

"No way to tell without examining her and maybe not even then. There's no end to the faces a sick mind can wear."

"Tell me about it," I said.

"You thinking of somebody in particular?"

"Yes." I told him who it was, and what had happened.

"You'll need proof."

"I know. I'm going after that tomorrow."

"Where?"

"Ricelander, for starters."

145

"That's way up north. And I hear there's a snow blowing in."

"When?" I thought we'd escaped with a near miss.

"Sometime tomorrow. It got stalled in the Rockies, but it's getting itself organized again."

"With any luck I'll beat it."

He smiled at that. He knew I didn't have any.

"I don't think Annie's faking it," I said.

"Is that your heart or your head talking?"

"Both."

He nodded. "That's a hard combination to beat. For what it's worth, I agree with you."

"It's worth a lot. So's your company right now."

"I'm sorry about Will. He and I went back a ways, too."

I turned to look into the fire. "That's where I'm having some trouble right now. I'm glad he didn't linger. And I'm glad he died with his boots on, fighting to save someone he loved. But I'm going to miss him, Doc. Every time an old friend dies my world gets a little smaller."

"Then make new friends."

"Easier said than done."

"But not impossible. Look at me, Garth, I'm eighty-two years old. Where would I be now if I just hung on to my old friends? Hell, I've buried nearly all of them, including Constance, my very best friend. That's the tough part about getting old. It's not the aches and pains, though they're bad enough. The good part is I've continued to make friends all along the way, and when the time comes, there'll be enough of them left to bury me."

"Just do me a favor, will you?" I said. "Wait another twenty years before you let that happen."

He smiled. There was a twinkle in his eye. "At least."

Later, at home, I made another call to Clarkie. This time he answered. "No, I haven't got a hold of Sheriff Roberts yet," he said. "I even sent him a telegram just in case. There's nobody there."

"That's okay. Keep trying. In the meantime try Kentucky to see if you can match those prints."

"Why Kentucky?"

"Call it a hunch. And the sooner the better."

"You mean tonight?"

"Yes. That's what I mean."

"Will do. Anything else?"

"Yes, unfortunately. Paul Peters and Will Cripe are dead."

"You know where they are?"

"Yes. They're under the old house on Hoover's Ridge. But I want them left there for now. Otherwise, we might spook their killer."

"You know who it is?"

"I think I do. Maybe by tomorrow I'll know for sure."

"What's tomorrow?"

"A long day."

But I wasn't even close.

16

Clarkie called early the next morning. But I was up already and had been for two hours. So had Ruth, who had limped downstairs to join me. Together we were on our second pot of coffee.

"I just heard from Kentucky," Clarkie said. "You were right. The prints on the pistol you found at Will Cripe's match those of a suspected murderer. They think he killed his wife, though they've never found her. After that he killed her lover and went off into the hills and hid. That's been over twenty years ago, and they haven't seen him since."

"What's his name?"

"Charles Summers is his real name. But his mother's maiden name was Lawson. They think he's used that in the past."

"Not anymore. Thanks, Clarkie. You can get some sleep now."

"That's not all. The way they tell it down there, this guy's some kind of mental case. On top of that, he's a crack shot and about as dangerous as they come. Proceed with all due caution, they said."

"I'll remember that," I said.

"Bad news?" Ruth asked when I hung up.

"It's not good news. Suspicions confirmed."

"Maybe you ought to stay here and not go to Ricelander."

"To what end? I can't get close enough to Annie to do any

149

good, and if I press Charles Lawson too close, he'll leave, then come after Annie another day when she's least expecting him."

"What good will going to Ricelander do you?"

"Establish his pattern. And destroy his alibi."

"Does he know you're getting close to him?"

"Yes. I think he does. He's too clever a man not to."

"Then you might be in as much danger as Annie."

"That also occurred to me. Another good reason to leave town today. I don't know exactly how his mind works, but I know enough to fear him."

"What do you think he plans to do?"

"Kill Annie if he can, then get out of here. He's been working toward that all week."

"From when on?"

"From the time he found Lucky digging in the abandoned house on Hoover's Ridge. My guess is that Lucky backtracked Annie to there, came across something that smelled interesting, likely a varmint of some kind, and started digging. Lucky couldn't know that the man who came up behind him was anything but a friend. Like Paul Peters, he never saw death coming."

"Why was Paul killed?"

"He loved Annie. He made the mistake of letting Charles Summers/Lawson know that."

"Does Charles Lawson know where Annie is staying?"

"Not exactly. But he's relentless. He could find her. Or," and this was my worst fear, "she might find him. Will Cripe's .30-.30 is missing. I think Annie took it."

"Then she knows her danger?"

"Yes and no. She knows she's in danger, but I'm not sure she knows yet who it is."

"And when she figures it out?"

"That's what I've got to keep from happening. And that's why I wish Rupert were here. I can't be two places at once."

"What about Clarkie?" Then she shook her head in self-reproach. "Forget I said that. That'd be like sending a turkey to stop a turkey shoot."

"They don't shoot turkeys at turkey shoots."

"In Clarkie's case they'd make an exception."

It was still dark when I reached Beulah Peters' house. Though I'd called her to tell her I was coming, she hadn't turned her Christmas lights on. That told me she'd already guessed my mission.

"Come in, Garth," she said on meeting me at the door. "I hope you don't mind that I'm not dressed."

She wore a black kimono over what looked like gold silk pajamas and brown hard-soled slippers that flopped as she walked. I followed her into the kitchen, where I sat at a small breakfast table under a blue lamp.

"Would you like coffee?" she asked, still standing.

"No thanks. I've been through two pots already."

She nervously rubbed her hands together and looked around the kitchen for something to do. Not finding anything, she turned back to me. "I know why you're here, Garth. It's to tell me that Paul is dead. But since I can't bear to hear that news, we'll pretend it isn't so. We'll talk about him in the present, not in the past. Then when you leave, taking my last hope with you, I'll sit down and have my cry."

I nodded. "Fair enough."

"So, aside from that, what news do you have for me?"

"A couple questions is all. Two weeks ago at Fair Haven Church, when Paul had played Annie's song, what did he do when he finished?"

"He got up and left. To have a cigarette, we all thought. But after he didn't come back, I went looking for him. I found him at the bottom of the basement steps."

"Was anyone else up and about?"

"I suppose they were in time. But not right away. Paul was . . . is the maestro, you see. He doesn't like it if he's there and we're not ready to sing."

"Where was Coop at the time?"

"In his office, I presume. That's where he usually is during choir practice."

"Did he come out at all?"

"When?"

151

"When Paul was playing Annie's song."

She thought about it for a moment. "He might have. Yes! I remember now. He burst out of his office, stared daggers at Paul, then went back in again."

"Are you sure?"

"Well, he went somewhere, I'm sure of that. He probably thought Paul had lost his mind, like the rest of us did."

"Or found it."

"What are you saying, Garth?"

"A hunch I have, one I'd ask Paul about if he were here."

"Why don't you ask me instead." She sat down across from me. For the moment her grief was forgotten.

"The other morning, when you came into the jewelry store, you said you and Paul had left some unfinished business at home. I assumed you were feuding over something. But that wasn't it. The feud didn't start until I showed you Annie's photograph. So what I'd like to know is, what was the unfinished business you started at home?"

"That's easy enough. I'd been telling Paul all along that Sommerville Cooper sounded familiar, that I was sure I'd heard him preach somewhere before, but I couldn't remember where. Paul asked me that morning at breakfast, sitting right there where you are now, if I might not have heard him here at Fair Haven Church."

"What did you say?"

"I said I didn't see how that was possible."

"Do you see now?"

"No. That's why I went in to see Paul at the jewelry store. I wanted to know what was going on, why he was acting the way he was. As his mother, I had a right to know."

"Thanks, Beulah. You will know in time."

"Why not now?"

"Because there's death in that knowledge."

"So what! I'm not afraid to die! With Paul gone . . ." She closed her eyes and clenched her fists, her entire body trembling as she did, "there's nothing to live for anyway."

I stood, but fought the urge to put my arms around her. It would have broken her if I had.

"Garth!" she called to me as I reached for the front door.

"Yes, Beulah?"

"Did Paul die in peace? God knows he had little enough of it while he was alive."

I thought it over. Like Will, Paul had died for love, trying to save Annie. Some might call that peace, which was good enough for me.

"Yes, Beulah, he died in peace."

"Thanks, Garth. It helps to know that."

Dawn was slow in coming and when it finally came, it didn't change much. It was grey everywhere I looked—grey fields and grey towns, grey slush on the highway, grey faces speeding by in grey cars. Grey inside too. No pretty thoughts wrapped in bright red ribbons.

Stopping once for gas, I reached Ricelander at mid-morning, just as it was starting to awaken. I turned right at a three-way stop and crossed a brownish river where a thick yellow foam floated amidst logs and debris. The foam belonged to a pulp mill and so did the smell it carried. To some it smelled like money.

I found the police office and a parking spot in front. The smell from the pulp mill followed me inside, but the man at the desk seemed not to notice.

He sat hunched over his typewriter, hunting and pecking his way through what looked like an accident report. The desk was piled high with papers, which had been pushed to one side to make room for the typewriter. Lean and weathered, the man had a look about him that said he'd spent most of his life out of doors and would never be happy behind a desk, even for a short time. I guessed he was somewhere in his mid-fifties.

"What do you need?" he asked, still pecking away.

"Some information."

"About what?"

"A revival. I hear you had one lately."

"You heard wrong. This is northern Wisconsin. About the only spirits you could revive here in December come in a bottle."

"That's what I thought."

"Who told you we were having a revival?"

"It's not important. Do you mind if I show your citizens a couple photographs, maybe ask a couple questions?"

"About what?"

"A case I'm working on."

"Name, rank, and badge number."

"I'm Garth Ryland. I publish the *Oakalla Reporter*."

He reached out and shook my hand without looking up. "Ken Birt, Chief of Police. I've read your column, even tried to get the paper here to carry it. No soap. The man who runs the paper says you're an anachronism, whatever the hell that is. But don't take it personal. He calls me the same thing." He finished with a flourish, rolled the report out of the typewriter, and dropped it on his desk. "Now, let's get the hell out of here before I find something else to do."

"Where are we going?" I asked.

"You said you had some questions to ask. You'll get a lot more answers if I'm along."

True to his word, Chief Ken Birt accompanied me all over town. But while I'd asked all my questions, I hadn't gotten any answers.

"It looks like this might be a dead end," I said. We were in his patrol car at the north end of town.

"Keep the faith," he answered. "I've got all day."

"I don't."

"We'll try one more place. If we don't have any luck there, we'll pack it in if you like."

"Fair enough."

We continued north out of town until we reached a crossroads, then turned east. About two miles later we came to a country church. It was a white wooden church with a high wooden steeple. Both needed paint.

"They call this church Fairview," Ken Birt said. "But I don't know what they're looking at."

He had a point. All I could see was snow, sand, and jack pine. Even on its best day, the view wouldn't get much better.

"Maybe it once was," I said, "a fair view."

"Not in my time. And I've been here forever."

"Is the church still active?"

"Far as I know. At least I haven't heard they've closed it down."

Beside the church was a log house with thick grey walls and a stone chimney. Low to the ground with only two small windows to let in the light, it had been built to withstand the icy winter winds that blew in from Lake Superior.

I knocked on the door. The man who answered it was thin and stooped and smelled like stale sweat. His house smelled the same way.

"Clarence, this is Garth Ryland from Oakalla," Ken Birt said. "He'd like to ask you a couple questions."

Clarence's eyes were small and bloodshot. He looked like he'd spent most of his life in a tunnel.

"Sure," he said.

I showed him a photograph I'd clipped from a September *Oakalla Reporter*. "Do you recognize this man?"

"Yep. He was here just a few months ago."

I handed him the gold locket Sam Licklightner had brought to me. "What about these people?"

He held it closer so he could see. I cringed as he did. His face and Annie's were inches apart. Then a wide smile creased his face. It looked like a leer to me.

"Annie!" he said. "Now there was a bed warmer."

I reached for the locket.

But he pulled back and wouldn't give it up. Something snapped inside me. I felt a ball of white rage ignite at the base of my skull. Had Ken Birt not stepped between us, I would have flattened Clarence.

Ken Birt took the locket from him and handed it to me. "Was there anything else you wanted to know?" he asked.

"Just one more question," I said. "Was the man in the locket here, too?"

"Clarence?" Ken Birt said when he saw Clarence wasn't going to answer.

"Stuff it," Clarence said. He nodded at either Charles Lawson or me. "Him, too, the bastard." Clarence went inside and shut the door.

"Sorry," I said when we got to the car. "I almost lost it."

"No harm done if you had. Most folks around here would thank you for taking a measure of Clarence."

"Still, that's not me."

"Been a tough week?"

"One of my toughest."

"You have a minute to spare?" he asked.

"That's about all I have, a minute."

We drove back toward Ricelander until we came to a stream, then got out of the patrol car and walked to its edge. The same stream I'd smelled in town raced through a gorge in a tumble and a roar, as its cold white water flung itself up at us. It didn't smell like pulp mill there. It smelled like wet pine.

"I always come here," he said above the rushing water, "whenever I need to wash off."

We stood for longer than a minute. We stood until my legs grew liquid and I could feel myself gliding down the rock to join the water below. Then we turned and walked to the car.

"Thanks," was the only thing said on our way back to town.

On the way home the sky began to lower and threaten snow. By the time I reached the farm, the first flakes had started to fall.

Inside the barn it was dark and quiet. No birds rustled on their perch. No cats darted for cover. With snow falling and night at hand, they should have been in there. It was a warning I didn't heed.

I turned on the light and climbed the ladder to the haymow. Annie's nest was cold. Her suitcase was still there, but when I opened it, I saw that her pencils and drawings were gone. Maybe she'd taken my advice and gone back to Four Corners.

Then I discovered Annie hadn't taken quite all of her drawings. The jackal with the man's face had been torn in two and left lying in the hay. Beside it lay Annie's drawing of the doe, her eyes no longer glazed with fear, but wide open with awareness and steeled with determination. I got the message. Tired of running, she had become the hunter. But what she didn't realize, and what put her in grave danger, was that she didn't have the heart to kill anyone. Charles Summers, on the other hand, did.

Piecing together the jackal with the man's face, I saw what Paul Peters had sensed and Will Cripe had seen, what he'd warned me about the night when he said a leopard couldn't change its spots. The man in Annie's drawing, the man who had stormed into my office when he saw his photograph in the *Oakalla Reporter*, and the man in the gold locket were all one and the same—Reverend Charles Summers/Lawson, or Coop, as I'd come to call him.

I took the drawings and started down from the haymow. My feet had just hit the floor when I felt something hard poke me in the kidney. It felt like the muzzle of a gun.

"Annie, is that you?"

No answer. But with Annie there wouldn't be.

I no longer felt the muzzle, so I slowly turned around. Will Cripe's .30-.30 Winchester was pointed at my chest. Annie was holding it.

"So we meet again," I said.

She didn't smile in greeting. She wore the same long black coat, the same pale skin, the same yellow hair. But like the doe's, her eyes had changed. No longer afraid, they looked at me with the full light of understanding.

"You know, don't you, who the danger is?" I asked.

She nodded ever so slightly.

"He struck you and left you for dead under the old house on Hoover's Ridge?"

She nodded again.

"And now that you know you're going to kill him," I said. "You can't, Annie. You don't have it in you. All you'll do is get yourself killed."

That angered her. She poked the muzzle of the Winchester at me. I understood. She wanted me to move.

"Where to?"

She nodded toward the door.

When we stepped outside, the storm descended upon us. In the near dark it was impossible to tell where the sky ended and the snow began.

Annie marched me to the food cellar just outside the back door of the house. The cellar was built of concrete and dug at least four feet into the ground. Except for its wooden doors, it would make a perfect bomb shelter.

I lifted the first door and started down the concrete steps. But then I balked at the whole idea. We weren't playing cops and robbers. Annie's life was in danger.

"Annie, listen to me," I said. "We've got the evidence to put Charles Lawson away for good. You don't have to prove how brave you are. I already know that. So why don't you just let me handle it from here?"

"No."

I barely heard her say it. At first I thought it was the wind mocking me. But when I turned and saw her anguish, how hard it had been to utter that one word, I knew she had spoken. Rather than destroy the moment and perhaps destroy her, I kept my peace, turned back, and finished my walk into the cellar.

Bang! The outside door slammed down. Then she latched it.

From boyhood I'd told Grandmother Ryland she needed a light in this cellar. For the past 6½ years I'd told myself the same thing. But since I used it so infrequently, I didn't think it mattered. Now it did.

Climbing the cellar steps on all fours until I reached the door, I gave it my best forearm shiver. The pain was sudden and complete. It shot through my right shoulder, down my right side, and left me weak in the knees. Several minutes passed before I could move my right arm again.

But a slow learner, I tried the same forearm shiver with my left arm, with nearly the same results. This time it felt like I'd broken my left wrist, along with every finger and knuckle on my

158

left hand. Again, minutes passed while I waited for it to stop hurting.

The next move wasn't easy because it put almost unbearable pressure on my right shoulder. But while lying on my stomach, I managed to point myself down the steps and hold myself there with my hands while I kicked at the door. Fortunately, I was wearing my leather work boots, and they gave some muscle to my blows. Gradually, though, my right arm began to buckle with the strain.

"Damn!" I yelled in frustration and kicked at the same time. That was all it took, a little extra effort. I felt the door give as I went sliding headfirst down the cellar stairs.

A shower of snow pelted me when I scrambled outside. I ran to Jessie, opened the door, and found my keys gone. I felt my pockets. The keys weren't there. I must have dropped them on the cellar steps.

That was my first thought. After searching the steps on my hands and knees, I realized Annie must have taken them. Nothing to do but make the long walk back to town.

17

It snowed and blew harder, the flakes so thick I could hardly see. No longer sheltered by the farm, I was at the mercy of the storm. It drove deep into my will, cut tears from my eyes and furrows in my face, and wrapped an icy scarf around my throat. Every step became a chore, each one heavier than the last. To break the monotony of pain, I began to run. Like the Little Engine that Could, the faster I ran, the better I began to feel. *I think I can. I think I can. I think I can.* My legs were no longer my own. They had their own will, their own rhythm, as relentless as the snow.

When I came to Fair Haven Road, I turned south toward town. Now at my back, the wind pushed me along, and the going was easier. I passed Fair Haven Church, which was all but obscured by the snow, and continued on. The way I now felt, I could run all night if I had to.

She appeared in the road coming toward me. Bent over and moving slowly, she left the road, floundered through the side ditch, then climbed the fence, hanging there a moment before she fell hard into the field on the other side.

That should have finished her. It didn't. A moment later she rose and plodded through the snow like some dull earthbound creature of the night, and so unlike the Annie I'd come to know.

I ran to where she'd crossed the fence. Kneeling, I saw the

problem. She had been hurt. The snow appeared dotted with blood.

Will Cripe's Winchester lay nearly buried in the snow beside the fence. I picked it up and brushed the snow from it. Working the action, I ejected a spent shell into my hand. Already I knew the story. Annie had her chance to kill him and missed, likely on purpose. Instead of the hunter she was back to being the hunted.

I smiled as I stroked the Winchester. At least the sides were even. But when I tried to work another shell into the chamber, it jammed on me and wouldn't budge no matter what I did. Nothing, when you really need it, is so worthless as a dead gun. I threw the Winchester back down in the snow.

Placing my footprints over Annie's, hoping the snow and wind would obscure them just enough to make them unreadable, I climbed the fence and followed her out into the bean field. When I reached mid-field, where the wind would be strongest, I stopped and waited, watching it erode her tracks until only a trace showed. Then I thought I heard the fence shake. Someone was crossing it where I had.

I walked north into the wind. Stopping once to look behind me, I could see a brown blur through the snow, growing larger as it came my way. He'd taken the bait. He was after me.

I walked faster. The woods ahead was one I knew well. If I could reach it with time to spare, I might put some distance between us.

At the edge of the woods I was stopped by an old wire fence. I didn't trust the fence to climb over it, but I didn't see any way through it. Climbing at the nearest post, which began to wobble under my weight, I was astraddle the fence when the post snapped and I went with it, riding it to the ground.

At impact I tried to roll away and got caught in a strand of barbed wire. It held me by the collar of my jacket, biting into my neck, as I lay helplessly on my back, watching the snow sift down.

Not a bad place to die. But not the place I'd choose. I lunged and pulled free, leaving some collar and skin behind.

Minutes later when I finally stopped to rest, I felt a warm trickle running down my back and into my shorts. I hoped it was sweat.

When I came to a stream, I turned east and began to follow it toward Willoby's Slough. As a boy I'd marveled at the stream's tenacity in fighting its way through the bends of the slough to eventually merge with the Wisconsin River, then the Mississippi, then the Gulf of Mexico. That night I marveled at its rock-ribbed clarity as it led me through the driving snow.

I returned to Fair Haven Road about a mile north of where I'd left it. Climbing the short steep grade to the road, I made sure I left tracks. At the top I was relieved to see someone had driven by recently.

Walking within the tire track, which hid my footprints, I went as far as the low iron bridge that crossed the stream. Bent and balanced on the ball of my right foot, I jumped and reached out for the bridge with my left foot, clearing the undisturbed snow. I caught a rail, but started sliding and nearly toppled backward before I threw myself against the bridge and hung on. As I did, I felt something tear in my chest. It momentarily took my breath away.

The next step was the hardest because I had to do it blind. I slid down the side of the bridge as far as I could go, hung by my hands, and dropped to the shallow water below. Only my hands saved me from an icy bath. But nothing could save my hands from going under. The shock of the cold water was like a slap on the wrist. It put everything in full focus and warned me of what might lie ahead.

A whistle ran under the bridge. Walking through it, I could hear my footsteps ricochet off its metal sides. It was peaceful in there, out of the wind and out of the snow, until I came to the other end and stepped back into the storm.

I followed the stream east, staying on top of rocks whenever possible. When I couldn't find a rock to step on, I had to wade in the water. Already my pants cuffs and the fingers of my gloves were frozen.

Where the stream bent south toward Willoby's Slough, I got out. From there on the pools were deeper, the footing less certain, and the danger from drowning very real. Looking west, I didn't see Charles Summers following. But in my bones I knew he was there.

I crossed a small woods and started through the cornfield on the other side. A stalk reached out and jerked me to the ground. I knelt, gasping for air. It felt like someone had driven an iron wedge through my chest.

Though I couldn't see them, I knew that to the south, the distant lights of Oakalla burned a halo in the snow. Faint and warm, like a fire's afterglow, they beckoned to me, said Garth, come on home.

I stared at the snow, unable to move. Tears came to my eyes. I was going to die there. "No!" I repeated Annie's first word to me. It was enough to get me going again. I headed directly for Willoby's Slough.

A tangle of cattail and saw grass lay ahead, and there was no way to reach the slough itself except through it. Wading in, I could hear the saw grass crinkle and crack, a brittle sheet metal sound that set my teeth on edge like nails drawn across a blackboard. It hurt my chest every step of the way.

Stumbling onto the ice, I fell to my knees, got up, and continued on. There was no way, in the snow, to read the ice—to know which was safe ice and which was not. I had to rely on my instinct to guide me. Aiming for the heart of the slough, I said a prayer to whoever might be listening and hoped for the best.

Minutes passed. I knew I was well into Willoby's Slough, but it seemed I hadn't moved at all. The sameness of the snow froze time and place and made each step seem circular, forever leading back upon itself. No landmarks measured my progress, only an occasional clump of grass that looked exactly like the clump of grass before.

But another dimension to Willoby's Slough remained in all seasons, regardless of the snow: its isolation. Out of the sight and sound of your fellow man, you were on your own. Normally I reveled in the thought. That night I dreaded it.

I barely heard the shot as the rifle ball tore through the

164

snow at my feet and bounced off the ice. I never looked back to see where the shot had come from. Charles Summers would have to reload his musket before he fired again. Time was of the essence.

Pushing deeper into the slough, I came to black ice, where the snow turned to slush as fast as it fell. I knew better than to go on, but I had come too far to turn back.

My heart pounded, filled with too many memories of black ice. I took a first step. The ice beneath the slush seemed solid. I took a second step and felt the ice give a little, like I'd stepped onto hard rubber. I held my breath. Nothing happened. Walking on tiptoe, feeling the ice sag with every step, I worked my way toward what I thought was good ice and safety. Almost there, I heard a shot and a shout and a splash. All came so close together that they came at the same time. They froze me in my tracks.

I turned to see where they had come from. That was a mistake. I could feel myself start to go down. Too late, I tried to turn back. I never made it. I slowly sank until I hit bottom, which left me chest deep in ice water.

At first I did nothing. There seemed nothing to do. Then the water cut through my jeans and into my legs. I tried to turn around and go forward, but the muck of the slough sucked at my boots and wouldn't let go.

Stork-like, I raised one leg, pivoted slowly, put it down and raised the other, falling forward on the ice as I did. I broke through, taking in a mouthful of marsh water, most of which ran into my lungs.

The fit of coughing that followed put the fight back in me and probably saved my life. Enraged, determined not to die there, with my next surge I flopped further up onto the ice and it held me. I crawled out of the water and took a moment to catch my breath.

In the quiet that followed I looked and listened for Charles Summers; saw and heard only the storm. An eerie feeling came over me. It said do not rejoice, for he has risen. I got up and started running.

At the first beaver lodge I turned west and didn't stop

165

running until I left Willoby's Slough behind. On the hill beyond, everything gave out at once, and I had to crawl the last few feet to the top.

Holding my chest, which seemed to be pulling apart rib by rib, I crossed a pasture to a fence. New, tightly strung, the fence looked about three-hundred feet high. I stood and stared dumbly at it, trying to wish it away. When it wouldn't go, I had to climb it.

I landed with a jar that should have hurt more than it did. No longer could I feel my toes, and my legs had a deep deadness to them that was inching toward my brain. I struggled through the side ditch onto Fair Haven Road. Somewhere ahead was Fair Haven Church. Warmth was there, and sanctuary, if I could reach it in time.

I tried to run toward it, to embrace the building that for me had become the very symbol of darkness. But my legs grew heavy, began to stumble under the weight of that knowledge. She is not there, something said to me. She is not there! To save her, you must go where she is.

I veered off the road, tumbled into the side ditch, and lay still. In the eternity that followed, I thought I heard footsteps approach and finally pass. Still I didn't move. With the wind rising and the snow falling ever harder, I wanted to stay where I was. And sleep. Perchance to dream.

18

I was cold. Not chilly-cold and uncomfortable, but brain-cold and in danger of freezing to death. When I reached Hoover's Ridge, I shook so hard I had to wrap my arms around a tree and hold on just to get control again.

Annie lay just inside the door of the abandoned house. I couldn't take her pulse. My hands were too cold. Gathering her into my arms, I carried her to the hearth, which held a breath of warmth.

Stirring the hearth with a piece of bark, I found a live coal beneath the grey mound of ashes. My hands trembled wildly as I tried to rip more bark from the pile of wood at my feet. I yelled in frustration. All I did was bloody my fingers.

I had to warm up. But my brain was too numb to think. I began beating my hands against my legs, trying to warm them. It gave me an idea. Holding my ribs with my right hand while I beat the air with my left, I began doing one-armed jumping jacks. I laughed out loud. If only Ruth could see me now.

But it worked. When my breathing slowed, I had enough control to splinter a few pieces of bark. I piled these on top of the coal and blew on them. A small yellow flame began to lick feebly at the bark. Cheered by my success, I blew harder, blew the flame out, and had to start all over.

Patience, I told myself. If I didn't get the fire started, we would freeze to death. I blew slowly and gently, letting the tiny

167

flame burn at its own pace. When it grew enough to add more bark, I did, then a small stick of wood when the bark caught fire. Whoever had laid in this wood knew what she was doing. It had saved my life. I only hoped I could save hers.

Taking the blanket from the chair, I spread it on the floor in front of the fire and put her on it. I unbuttoned her coat to look at her wound and discovered it wasn't as bad as I'd feared. The ball from Charles Summers' musket had grazed her right side, but it didn't appear to have hit anything vital. She was suffering from shock and exhaustion more than anything else.

I took off her dress and tore strips from it to wrap her wound. She whimpered but didn't wake up. Turning my attention to the fire, I added as much wood as I thought the hearth could stand. Once the fire blazed, I undressed, then hung my clothes up to dry. Shaking the snow from her coat, I put it on top of the blanket and wrapped the blanket around us. Then I took her in my arms and held on tight.

The storm continued. I could feel the wind buffet the walls, see cannons of snow burst against the window, while the trees raked back and forth along the eaves, like they were scratching at the house, wanting in. But they wouldn't get in. No one would. Whatever danger lurked outside, it wouldn't find us there.

The first time Annie awoke, it was with a start. Panic momentarily showed in her eyes as she tried to twist away from me. But I wouldn't let go of her. And once she saw who I was, she stopped struggling.

"How are you feeling?" I asked.

She just looked at me.

I started to get up. She grabbed hold of me and held me back.

"I've got to feed the fire," I said. "I won't be gone long."

I got up and added some more wood. As soon as I was back in the blanket, she was back in my arms. She snuggled against me, sighed, and went back to sleep.

But I couldn't sleep. The events of the past week kept

running through my mind. I tried to piece them together as best I could, but I would need Annie's help to finish.

The next time she awakened there was a question in her eyes.

"He's dead," I said. "He drowned in the slough." At least that's what I wanted to believe.

She closed her eyes and turned away.

That angered me. I thought she would be happy to hear he was dead.

"He was a monster, Annie, a man-jackal. You have no reason to grieve for him."

When she turned back, there were tears in her eyes. She touched her finger to my lips for silence. I got the message. I wasn't to tell her for whom to grieve.

"I'm sorry," I said. "I once liked him too."

She held up two fingers. For a moment I thought she was giving me the peace sign; then I realized what she was saying.

"Yes," I said. "He was two different people."

She put her hand gently on my chest.

"At heart," I added for her sake. Then I asked, "When did it come to you who he was?"

She struggled with the word and finally said, "Today."

"You came back here and it all came back to you?"

She nodded, then pointed at the floor.

"You saw what was beneath it?"

She tried to speak, but couldn't. The horror was too much for her.

"I'm sorry, Annie."

She shuddered and drew close to me again.

More time passed. The storm continued, but its pace was less frenzied, its snow-volleys lighter than before. I checked our wood supply, saw we had more than enough to last the night, and wished I could will time to stop. With Annie beside me, there was no need to go anywhere else. And tomorrow it would all end.

I got up and fed the fire. Annie rested on one elbow,

watching me. On my return she held the blanket for me as I crawled in beside her.

"How's your side?" I asked.

She nodded.

"Okay?"

She nodded again.

"We'll get you to the hospital tomorrow."

She shrugged as if to say she was in no hurry.

I lay watching the fire. She lay watching me. Neither one of us was sleepy.

"Do you mind answering a few questions?" I asked. "It might be my last chance to ask them."

She thought it over. As she did, my gaze stayed on the fire. It ranked right up there with the best I'd ever built.

"Well?" I said.

She nodded. It was my turn.

"Did you see Charles kill Will Cripe?"

She shook her head no.

"But you did see him while he was there at Will's house, and he followed you, but you escaped from him."

She nodded, then made a blank face.

"You saw him, but you didn't know who he was or why he was following you. But there was something familiar about him. That's why you went back later and took Will's rifle. You felt an old danger."

She smiled and touched her hand to my head.

"Thanks," I said. "I think I'm smart too."

She laughed, then took my hand and patted me on the back.

"Okay," I said. "I deserved that."

She was still smiling at me. I found it hard to concentrate on the questions I had.

"What about Will Cripe?" I asked. "Were you once in love with him?"

Her face grew somber. That wasn't an easy question to answer, especially after eight years and everything that had happened since.

"Okay. We'll move on."

But she caught my arm as if to say wait. She wanted to try to explain. She did so by pointing to the fire, then her feet, which she wiggled to imitate walking, then the snow at the window. I understood. It was like Will had said. She and he loved the same things.

"What about Paul Peters? Did you love him?"

She looked confused. The name didn't register.

"Paul Peters," I said. Then I wriggled my fingers. "He played the piano."

She wriggled her fingers back at me. I thought she still didn't understand. Knowing Annie, I should have known better.

"Paul Peters," I said, raising my voice a little. "He played the piano at the Fair Haven Church."

Her look said in no uncertain terms she knew that. Then she wriggled her fingers again, this time across my chest hard enough for it to hurt.

"I give up," I said.

But she didn't give up. Exasperated, she assumed Paul's pose, the look of total concentration he'd had whenever he played the piano. Then she began playing my chest again, not looking at me the whole time.

In self-defense I came up with part of the answer. "You respected his talent . . ." Quickly she opened my hands, then slowly closed them, squeezing them tight at the end. "But he held it too close, kept his light under a bushel."

She made a fist and struck herself hard in the chest.

"Like you?"

She nodded.

"That's not true, Annie! I've heard you sing. I know what you can do."

She gave me a stern look, though the corners of her mouth turned upward in a smile.

"Okay, I'll shut up. You know who you are. You don't need me to defend you."

She lightly touched my chest, letting her hand rest there.

"Yeah, I know," I said. "My heart's in the right place."

171

We lay for a while without talking. She was so light and easy to hold that it was hard to tell where she ended and I began. And all of my hurts seemed to dissolve into her being. I hoped it was the same for her.

"Annie, I have to tell you something, because I think it's something you should know. Will and Paul both loved you. And I think what would matter most to them now is that you are safe. You understand that, don't you? Had I died tonight trying to save you it would have been worth it to me." I reached over to stroke her hair. "Because I love you, too. I know I'll never have you. Life is neither that kind nor that cruel. But I know you exist, even among and in spite of the Charles Summerses of the world, and that's all that matters."

Her eyes said she wasn't going to answer. She put her hand on my chest, then ran it the length of my body, as if appraising me to see what art she might find there. Very little, I assumed. Naked or loinclothed, I really wasn't statue material.

"Well?" I said.

She shook her head.

"I didn't think so."

She bit her lip to keep from laughing.

"What's so funny?"

But she never told me. She gathered me in her arms and held me close. Without making love, it was the sweetest love I ever made.

Awakening with a start, I didn't know where I was; then when I did know, I was suddenly afraid. I tried to rise and couldn't. It felt like my chest had grown to the floor.

Sitting, I looked around the darkened room. The fire was a bed of coals, the window pale with dawn's first light. Snow sifted down through a crack in the ceiling, dripping white dust on the floor. But where was Annie?

"Annie!" I yelled.

She turned from the fire. She'd been there all along. A smudge of soot on her face, dressed in the remains of her green gabardine dress, she looked like Cinderella.

"Aren't you cold?" I asked.

She smiled shyly at me.

I covered her with her coat, then dressed in front of the fire. My clothes had dried in the night. Though a little crusty, they felt snug and warm.

She watched me all the while. Her eyes were bold and curious, like those of a cat. She'd come a long way this past week. For that matter, so had I.

"Time to go," I said.

She just sat there.

"Annie, we can't stay here. Either one of us."

She cocked her head and looked at me, a smile playing at the corners of her mouth.

173

"Damn you," I said. "Why do you have to make it so hard?"

She rose and put on her coat. Then she picked up her packet of drawings and we were ready to go.

Outside, the snow had stopped, but a slate sky and a bitter northeast wind said it would soon return. There were at least eight inches of new snow on the ground. It had fallen in drifts and scallops that looked too sculptured to be real.

I watched Annie's eyes as she surveyed the woods. She delighted in its newness and, like me, hated to be the one who marred it. She glanced at me, asking if we could turn back. I shook my head no.

We descended from Hoover's Ridge, crossed Fair Haven Cemetery, and stopped in the churchyard. I saw no tracks leading in or out of the church.

Annie noticed me looking and glanced up at me with a question in her eyes.

"Nothing," I said. "Let's go."

When we reached Fair Haven Road and started south toward town, the road had already been plowed. In one way I was thankful. The going would be much easier than it would have been otherwise. In another way I was sorry. When the snow had lain white and untouched, the morning had belonged to just Annie and me. Then it no longer did.

Annie felt it, too. Unable to contain her joy, she had raced ahead of me, broken through a drift, and fallen down, then needed my help to get out again. Or pretended to need it, so she could drag me laughing down on top of her.

Along Fair Haven Road, however, she trudged beside me with her head down and her steps measured and her hands in her pockets. To make it official, Clarkie met us in his patrol car before we'd gone a hundred yards.

"Garth! You're alive!"

I looked at Annie and smiled. "Very much so."

"I've been out all night looking for you. So has Ruth, most of it anyway. Where were you?"

"With a friend. Do me a favor, will you, Clarkie? Run Annie to the hospital for me. There's somewhere I have to go."

Annie looked at me with surprise, then alarm.

"It's okay," I said. "Clarkie's a good man. He won't let anything happen to you."

She made a fist and hit me hard in the chest. That hurt. She'd hit me right in my sore spot.

"Damn it, Annie! I said you'd be all right."

Then she pointed at me, and I understood.

"I'll be all right, too," I said. "Clarkie's coming back to pick me up as soon as he gets you admitted. I'll see you there shortly."

She wasn't reassured. And when I opened the door for her, she wouldn't get into the patrol car. I had to lift her in and close the door behind her.

"What happens when we get to the hospital?" Clarkie said.

"Take her to emergency. She has a wound that needs to be cleaned and bandaged."

"I mean if she won't get out on her own."

"That's your problem. I got her in."

When I waved goodbye to Annie, she stuck her tongue out at me. I had to laugh.

But my mood changed on my return to Fair Haven Church. If Charles Summers had walked past me while I lay in the ditch last night, he had likely gone there. If he had gone there, then he hadn't left.

Inside the church it was nearly as cold as it was outside. Watching my breath rise, balloonlike, up the bell tower, I knew that had I gone to the church neither Annie nor I would have survived the night. Not something to dwell on, but something to keep in mind.

I went down to the furnace room at the north end of the basement. The furnace was cold and the pilot light was out. Either the wind had blown it out or the outside fuel line had frozen in the storm. Whatever the case, Fair Haven Church needed help.

I called Bill Gaylord and told him the problem. He said he'd have an oil truck there within the hour. I smiled as I set down the receiver. It was nice to have connections.

After searching the church from basement to sanctuary, I

still had the feeling Charles Summers was there. From the moment I entered the church, his shadow hung over me like a black bubble. It pressed down with the cold and attached itself to my soul, then lifted again the moment I stepped outside.

From the church I walked to Will Cripe's house and went over the hill into Willoby's Slough. Peacefully white, the slough was broken by neither man nor beast. I thought I knew where I'd gone through the ice. But I couldn't make myself move in that direction. Instead, I turned up the collar on my sheepskin jacket, put my hands in my pockets, and started home. Clarkie met me part way there and took me the rest of the way.

"It's about time!" Ruth said when I hobbled in the back door. "Where in the world have you been?"

"Why? Did you miss me?"

"Like a toothache." She helped me out of my jacket, then poured me a cup of coffee as I sat down at the kitchen table. "You'd better call Clarkie. He's worried sick."

"There's no need. He brought me home."

"From where?"

"The abandoned house on Hoover's Ridge. Annie Lawson and I spent the night there."

"Doing what?"

"Surviving."

"You smell like you slept in a chimney."

"I imagine I look even worse."

"No. You look pretty good considering." She gave me the once over. "Is there a reason for that?"

"Heredity."

"I mean why you're smiling."

"I didn't realize I was."

"From ear to ear. I don't suppose Annie Lawson has anything to do with that."

"No. Nothing at all."

"Then why don't you tell me about it and let me decide for myself."

So I told her how my night had gone. Most if it, anyway. She could guess the rest.

176

"Then you don't know whether Charles Summers is dead or not," she said when I finished.

"No. I wouldn't want to bet either way."

"Did you go back to Fair Haven Church to look?"

"There and Willoby's Slough both. But I couldn't make myself go back out onto the ice. If he's there, somebody else will have to find him."

"Does that bother you?" she asked.

"What? That I couldn't go back out onto the ice?"

"Yes."

"No. I'll be able to in time. But not soon and not alone, the way I used to. There's nothing more I need to prove there."

"It sounds like you're getting smarter in your old age."

"I've been telling you that all along."

She got up and poured us each another cup of coffee. I noticed she had dark circles under her eyes. Clarkie was right. She hadn't gotten much sleep last night either.

"So what are you worried about then?" she asked. "Even if Charles Summers did survive the storm, what are his chances of ever finding Annie again?"

"Annie's home is Kentucky. I'm sure she'll go back there now. If she has anything to go back to?"

"She does. We finally located her parents. They're not as old as I figured or as backward as everyone had me believe. They just don't like phones, so they don't own one."

"There are days I wish I didn't."

"Amen to that. But I still don't understand why you think Annie will still be in danger. I'd think that Kentucky is the last place Charles Summers would go."

"He came back here, didn't he? For some reason he keeps repeating himself. I don't know why. Whether it's his ego trying to get away with it, or some twisted attempt to undo the harm he's done, or that he really is two different people, and the right hand doesn't always know what the left hand is doing. I'm sure he sent those letters to himself, and wrecked his own office at the church. What would be the point, unless it was Charles Lawson reasserting himself again after eight years." It made sense to me, but Ruth's look said she had her doubts.

"You think Charles Lawson went into hiding after he thought he'd killed Annie?"

"I'm sure he did. And had plastic surgery while he was at it. It was the only way he could hide his scar."

"What about his hair? It went from black to white if I remember right."

"Over eight years that could have happened naturally, especially if he'd dyed it black before. He was a wanted fugitive in Kentucky. Perhaps he'd already altered his appearance before he ever came here."

"And the water in his gas, what about that? Right hand or left, no man is crazy enough to pour water into his own gas tank, then blame it on somebody else," she said, sure she had me.

"No. I don't think he did. I think it's like Sniffy Smith said. Coop always kept his tank so low the water probably condensed in there. But with everything else that was happening, Coop naturally blamed it on somebody else. Paul Peters probably. Though Paul didn't realize it at the time, he was the one who recalled Charles Lawson by playing Annie's song that night at the church."

"How did he know to play it?"

"I don't know, Ruth. His hands knew, and as Paul said, the music came whether he willed it or not."

She rubbed her arms to warm them. "Sounds spooky to me."

"You'll get no arguments there."

The phone rang. Clarkie was on the other end. "Garth, in all the excitement I forgot to tell you. Sheriff Roberts won't be coming home anytime soon. He's snowbound in Omaha."

"Where's he been? Did he say?"

"Denver. They barely beat the storm back."

"Denver! What in the world was he doing there?"

"You'll have to ask him."

"I plan to the first chance I get. Did you find Coop's purple De Soto?"

"Yes. It was in his garage, packed and ready to go, like you

178

said it'd be. When I opened the trunk, I found a tire iron inside and what looked like dried blood on it. Blood inside the trunk, too, and what I think is human hair."

"It probably belongs to Will Cripe and Paul Peters. Find a new parking place for that De Soto, Clarkie. I don't want it to suddenly turn up missing."

"Will do. Anything else?"

"If you're not too tired, round up some help and go out to Willoby's Slough before it starts snowing again. Be sure to take your wet suit and plenty of rope. If Charles Summers is there, he'll be about a mile southeast of Will Cripe's house."

"I'll get on it right away. In the meantime, you might call Sheriff Roberts. The last time I talked to him, I was pretty well convinced you were dead."

"He should know better. But I'll get around to it sometime today."

I hung up and started to put on my coat and cap.

"Where are you going?" Ruth asked.

"The hospital. I want to see how Annie is."

"I'd think you'd know by now."

"Correction, I want to see Annie."

"That's better."

As I walked to the hospital, it started to snow again. But I was walking with the wind and hardly felt it. At the entrance to the parking lot I saw an old blue Dodge leaving as I was coming in. The driver looked familiar, but I couldn't place her. What intrigued me more were the Dodge's heavy bumpers and the chains on the tires. This was a car that could drive through an avalanche.

I went in the emergency entrance, where I was a familiar figure of late. The nurse on duty took one look at me and said, "You just missed her."

My heart sank. "Missed whom?"

"Annie Lawson. She just left."

"Why didn't you stop her!" I yelled.

"For what reason? We did all we could for her, all that needed to be done. She's fine. You don't have to worry."

"You just let her walk out of here alone?" I still couldn't believe she was really gone.

"No. Not alone. Someone came after her."

"Who?"

"I'm not sure. A Mrs. Gohler, I believe. Annie wrote down the message and we made the call for her."

I started outside. Maybe I could catch them before they left town.

"Garth?"

"Yes?"

"Annie left these here for you." She handed me my keys and Annie's drawing of the timber wolf.

I looked at the drawing of the wolf. He knew what I was thinking. His smile said as much. Then I lowered the drawing and tapped myself on the heart. "That's the reason you should have stopped her. It's broken."

The nurse tapped her own heart in imitation of Annie. "I know. So was hers."

20

Christmas Eve. Ruth and I sat in front of the fire drinking whiskey-and-eggnog and toasting our newly decorated Christmas tree. That afternoon we'd buried Paul Peters and Will Cripe in Fair Haven Cemetery. Using Will's shovel, the one I'd used to bury Lucky, I'd tossed the first shovelful of dirt onto his coffin. I was glad I'd cleaned it for him.

A short while after he called, Clarkie and several men from town had gone to Willoby's Slough in search of Charles Summers, but either he wasn't there or they couldn't find him. The snow on Sunday and the sub-zero cold that followed Monday and Tuesday had put an ice cap on Willoby's Slough that probably wouldn't melt until spring. There was nothing we could do but wait until it did.

I had Ruth's present to me in my lap and she had my present to her in hers. I hadn't opened mine yet. There was no need to. Every year she bought me a flannel shirt from the five and dime there in Oakalla. The only thing in question was the color.

I picked up the box and shook it.

"It's a flannel shirt," she said.

"What color?"

"Open it and find out."

I tore off the wrapping paper and opened the box. The shirt was green and black. I decided to put it on. "What do you think?" I asked when I came back into the room.

"I like it or I wouldn't have bought it."

"So do I. Thanks, Ruth."

"You're welcome."

I sat down and watched her open my present to her. Once she got the moccasins out of the box, the first thing she did was hold them up to the fire to look at them.

"Try them on," I said.

"I'm getting to that. I just wanted to see where they were made."

"Wisconsin. Not very far from here."

"By Indians?"

"You have my word on it."

Satisfied, she tried them on and left them on, which was a major victory for me. "So where are you off to tonight?" she asked.

"Fair Haven Church. They're holding a short service there. You're more than welcome to come along."

She shook her head. "No, I think I'll stay home tonight. Drink an eggnog for Karl. Get to bed early."

I glanced at Diana's present under the tree. "Both of us, it looks like."

After putting on my jacket and stocking cap, I stood for a moment admiring the tree. Then I picked up Diana's present and started for the door. As I was going out, I met Rupert coming in.

"You're back," I said.

"You knew I was back. I told you so last night."

"That's right, you did. Sorry to spoil your vacation."

"What was there to spoil?" He spat in disgust. "I couldn't drink and I couldn't chew, and I had to eat at eight, noon, and five whether I was hungry or not. On top of that they kept a long-haired cat in the house that eats better than I do."

"I'm sorry to hear that. As you know, you sure missed a great time here."

"Why didn't you call me sooner?"

"We tried. You weren't there. Besides, Clarkie and I had a handle on it the whole time. I think he's underpaid."

"So he tells me. Seriously, Garth, how bad was it?"

"Seriously, Rupert, you don't want to know."

"Any chance Charles Summers is still in Oakalla?"

"I wouldn't bet against it." Then I reached into my jacket pocket and handed him a sack of his favorite chewing tobacco. "Merry Christmas," I said.

To my surprise, he reached into his pocket and handed me a small gold nugget. "Merry Christmas to you, too."

I held it up to watch the lights play off of it. Except for the wedding ring I no longer had, it was the only gold I'd ever owned. "Where did you get it?" I asked.

"Denver. That's what we went there for. At least that was my excuse to get out of the house."

"Thanks. I really like it."

"You could look happier about it," he said. "Particularly since they brought the cat along in my car."

"The next time we have a week, I'll tell you about it."

"You need a ride anywhere?"

"No. If I can get Jessie to start, I'm on my way to Fair Haven Church."

"Then light a candle for me."

"I'll be sure to."

At her Christmas best Jessie started on the first try. Driving out Fair Haven Road, I could see Venus, bright in the western sky. I thought of the Wise Men and their star and how beautiful it would be if it were true.

A few of the faithful had gathered at the church, people like Ben and Sissy Pickering who, through their hard work and heartfelt devotion had kept the church alive over the years. Beulah Peters was there, too, looking as sad as I felt. I took a seat beside her. She smiled, said "Hello, Garth," then offered to share her hymnal.

I liked the simple service. Ben Pickering read from the Book of Matthew the story of Christ's birth. Then each of us lit a candle, the lights were turned out, and we sang "Silent Night."

Watching the candlelight burn back the shadows, smiling as Annie's pure sweet voice joined that of Beulah's to fill the church with song, I knew I had come home again, that Fair Haven

183

Church had survived its time of darkness and would from that time forward grow toward the light.

When the music ended, it truly was a silent night. No one dared move, afraid to break the spell. Finally Ben Pickering stepped down from the pulpit, blew out his candle, and left. Others followed. Soon I sat alone in the sanctuary.

But for the longest time I couldn't move. I didn't want to move and leave this feeling behind. In all my years of believing, then doubting, then warring, then finally making my peace again, it was the closest I'd ever been to God.

I blew out my candle and walked out into the vestibule, where I turned on the light. "You can come down now, Annie," I said into the bell tower. "Everyone else has gone."

I waited for her to appear. When she didn't, I said "Annie, this is Garth. Don't play games with me."

This time when she didn't answer, I started up the ladder after her. On the first few rungs it was warm in the tower, warmer even than the vestibule. But the warmth was deceiving. Midway up the tower began to cool, and like Dante's *Inferno*, each step thereafter was colder than before.

"Annie," I said, "it's cold in here. Don't make me climb all the way to the top."

No answer. I climbed on.

When I reached the top, I already knew Annie wasn't there. But Charles Summers was. He lay on his right side, wedged into the tiny alcove at the top of the tower. One arm was tucked at his side, the other stretched out in front of him. He appeared to be reaching out for someone, but for whom I didn't know.

As I knelt to close his eyes, I noticed the faint outline of the scar on his cheek. It had bloomed in death, assumed the shade of the cold white moonlight that poured down upon it. Fascinated, I was in the act of tracing it when I stopped myself. Charles Summers was dead. That was all the truth I needed.

I climbed back down the ladder and into the vestibule. Annie waited for me there. She wore her long black coat, a hint of makeup, and small gold earrings that matched her hair.

"You look lovely, Annie," I said.

She smiled in reply.

"Thanks for the drawing. It was my favorite."

She nodded. She already knew.

"So where do you go from here?"

"Home." She didn't stutter. She'd been practicing the word.

"Kentucky?"

She nodded.

"How will you get there? Edith Gohler?"

She nodded again. Then she ran to me and threw herself into my arms. I held her momentarily, then let her go.

Outside, one of those cold and crusted December nights pinched my nose and dazzled me with all of the stars in the sky. Looking across Fair Haven Cemetery toward Hoover's Ridge, I saw a small solitary figure make her way toward the road. She seemed to float as she walked, like a nightingale barely skimming in the snow, growing fainter until I couldn't see her at all.

21

A light burned inside Diana's house. I knocked on the front door. A moment later she opened it. She wore grey wool slacks that matched her eyes and a grey-and-white ski sweater that matched her slacks. She was the perfect match tonight . . . as always.

"What? No hug?" She asked as I stepped inside.

I took a long look at her and felt all the things I'd felt since the first day I saw her. I could never deny her, not matter where we went or what we did or how far apart we seemed to grow. But at the moment I was going to try.

"I brought you your present," I said. "I wanted to give it to you in person." I tried to hand it to her. She wouldn't take it.

"I've built a fire," she said. "I want you to sit with me beside it. Then I'll open my present after you've opened yours."

I looked at her. I looked outside where I'd been. It suddenly seemed a lot colder out there. I closed the door behind me.

As she took my jacket, she saw me wince. "What's the matter?" she asked.

"I hurt my ribs."

"You want to tell me about it?"

"Maybe later."

We went into the family room where the fire was. She could do about anything she tried to do, except build a fire. It was smoking badly. I opened the screen and went to work.

187

Meanwhile she brought us each a glass of brandy. "I like your shirt," she said. "Is it from Ruth?"

"Who else."

"How is she?"

"About the same as always. You know Ruth."

She smiled. Whenever she did, I always felt like smiling too. "Yes, I know Ruth. I don't think I'm her favorite person."

"You used to be. Before you met me."

"That's what I mean. I think she thinks I don't do right by you."

"You don't."

"Let's not get into that tonight, please."

I sat watching the fire. I'd turned the tide. It was no longer smoking and in a few minutes it would be burning well. "What made you decide to come home?" I asked. "Or should I guess? Your friend Devin is married. He wanted to be with his family tonight."

"You're right on one count," she said. "Devin is married. But he wanted to be with me tonight. I told him I wanted to be with you."

"I guess I should feel honored."

That hurt her. I wasn't surprised. I'd intended for it to. "It's not too late to change my mind," she said.

I didn't answer. Instead, I sat watching the fire. She came to sit beside me.

"Garth, it's Christmas Eve," she said. "Let's not argue. It never gets us anywhere. You want me here. I can't be here and still be myself. What's the point in beating ourselves over the head with it? Why can't we accept it and go on from there?"

"Because it's damn hard to love a memory."

"That's all I am to you—a memory?"

"When you're not here, what else is there? Once your house is sold . . . I don't even want to think about that."

"I hardly ever use my house anymore. And I don't know when I'll use it again. It makes sense to sell it now while I can."

"Not to me."

188

"That's because you're seeing it through your heart, not your mind."

"Where you're concerned my heart and mind are in the same place. Always have been, always will be. Don't expect me to love you in any other way."

She glanced up in exasperation. Then she took hold of me and began to shake me. "Damn you! Why must you be so stubborn!"

I reached out and put my arms around her. She was still trying to shake me but not getting very far. After a while she quit altogether and let me hold her. She felt good to hold. I'd almost made myself forget how good.

"This doesn't solve anything," she said.

"I know. But it feels good."

"No more talk about us," she said.

"No more talk about us," I agreed.

"So," she said pulling away. "It's time for you to open your present. It's in the bedroom. I'll have to go get it."

"Do I get to come along?"

She smiled her evil smile. "Whenever you want."

"After we've opened our presents."

"I think I can wait that long."

I watched the fire. It'd come full flame and warmed me where I sat. I stretched out on the rug in front of it and let myself go.

Diana returned with my present. She even helped me open it. It was *Mrs. Peter Rabbit,* a children's book by Thornton W. Burgess. It was also a first edition with the dust jacket still on.

"How did you know this was my favorite?" I asked.

"I guessed. Peter is a hopeless romantic. He sounded the most like you."

"You know me well."

Her eyes were shining. "I know."

I picked up her present and handed it to her. She had the wrapping off in about two seconds. When she lifted the necklace out of the box to look at it, her face told me all I needed to know.

"Where did you find it?" she asked, putting it on.

"That's a trade secret. But it's the genuine article. I'll vouch for that."

She kissed me, then again once she had my attention. "So are you, the genuine article."

"You know what I'm thinking," I said.

"What's that?" Though she already knew.

"I'm thinking how good you'll look with just your necklace on."

"I can hardly wait to show you."

I raised my glass and touched it to hers. "Merry Christmas."

"Merry Christmas."